THE SAGA
OF
NELIA DOE

By

William D. McCann

NEWGRANGE PRESS

ISBN 10 – 0976801116
EAN 13 – 9780976801115

Authored by William D. McCann
www.wdmccann.com

Cover artwork by Richard W. DeRosset
www.richardderosset.com

Celebrating the heroism of
immigrants everywhere
and
dedicated to
those who selflessly battle
oppression and injustice.

§

"There is no great genius
without some tincture of madness."

~

LUCIUS ANNAEUS SENECA

Disclaimers

UNITED STATES OF AMERICA

This is a work of fiction. Although for the sake of verisimilitude, the names of certain people are used in the book, their use is fictional and the interactions with the characters the author has invented are wholly the author's creation and are not intended to be understood as description of real or actual events, or to reflect in any way upon the actual conduct or character of these real people.

UNITED KINGDOM AND THE EUROPEAN UNION

In this work of fiction, the characters, places, and events are either the product of the author's imagination or they are used entirely fictitiously. Any resemblance to actual persons, living or dead, is purely coincidental.

Book One

CHAPTER I

IN THE HILLS OF BEVERLY

The glassine magic carpet of your imagination is a cozy place from which to experience this story. Imagine yourself in the Bois de Boulogne. The leaves of the elms, dampened by the first rain of the season, begin to fall. You are drinking a lovely sancerre on a slightly damp zinc table, staring into the eyes of a loved one.

This is essentially a love story, and love is deep, mysterious, and often unknowable; like the ninety percent of a glacier, which lies below the surface, these pages merely reflect the tale's hidden parts, which you must discover in your own subconscious. So now, gently launch yourself in the counter-clockwise flow of time, across the river of passion and pain, carried by the cosmos.

Imagine a toddler slowly, and painfully, dog paddling the length of a swimming pool. Were you a raptor circling above, the pool would appear as a topaz set in a baguette of emerald foliage.

A white uniformed nanny, venerable by her references and tinted blue hair, with one hand adjusts a pashmina to protect her wattles against the sun. The other holds open an article knifing the Princess of Wales. The former Nanny of Prince Charles might be forgiven her delight in the tabloid had she noticed the child faltering.

An aluminum splinter deflates a water wing supporting the child's left arm; he inhales a draught of chlorinated water.

Perhaps the projectile originated somewhere over Alaska, a sliver from a fanjet blade of an Airbus 300, floating in the jet stream for a thousand miles or so before falling to earth in Beverly Hills. Perhaps it has been propelled by someone lurking in the dense shrubbery thought to privatize the pool. However launched, later forensic examination determines its provenance as aircraft grade aluminum.

When the child stops kicking, his legs swing beneath him. The water wing on his right arm floats free as he descends toward the pool's drain. He claws at the liquid closing over his head as if reaching for an apple, a movement so feeble it barely ripples the surface, an immersion so swift there is no time to cry for help.

At the far end of the pool, behind the unvigilant nanny, a tall, muscular black woman, dressed only in tee shirt, fringed Levi cutoffs, and flip-flops, sees the child submerge. She dashes past the Nanny, dives into the deep end, reaches for the child's corn silk hair. In one continuous move, she hoists him above the surface of the water and onto the deck. She vaults from the pool. Dangling him by his ankles with one strong arm, she crushes him to her breast with the other, squeezing water from his lungs as if from a sponge.

Nanny discards Princess Di, gaping in walleyed shock as streams of water cascade from a curtain of long curly hair concealing the boy. He sputters, coughs, and begins to wail.

The woman rights the boy, cradles him, and croons:

> *"Valentina, Valentina*
> *Rendido estoya tus pils*
> *Se me han matar mañana*
> *Que me maten de una vez"*

The nanny calculates how to conceal this incident. She tries to dismiss the woman, an employee of an outside pool cleaning service, who refuses to relinquish the sobbing child, silencing the old lady with a venomous look.

Subconsciously the child knows he is the victim of yet another nanny, the sixth in a series of deposed caregivers. He has lost more weight during this one's tenure than with the others.

The boy's father unexpectedly arrives at poolside to observe his son's exercises. At first, he believes a kidnapper has got his son by the legs. Then he focuses on the woman's strange, feline eyes. They scare him. They look through him and past him, yet, tell him everything he needs to know. It is as if he isn't there, doesn't matter.

While Nanny blurts her excuses, he presses a button on the pool phone, summons his personal security waiting in the limo nearby. They escort the sputtering old hen from the premises.

As Nanny is led away, the black woman slowly shifts her gaze to the walls of foliage, their variations of green, the way the light colors certain leaves yellow, others jade, or amaranth, a patterning which, in her childhood, could predict a good or bad day, distinguish truth from lies, and invariably have something interesting to say about death.

She knows that her life will now change. For the better, who could say?

A storyteller capable of entertaining American audiences with seven hours of prime time brain candy each week, the boy's father has no trouble distinguishing fact from fiction.

He hasn't a clue who this woman might be, or where she came from, but his son, cradled in her arms, looks as though he has come home, at last.

Those are the circumstances under which Nelia Villa Lobos became the nanny of Sandy Golden, the only son of Andrew Golden, the most successful producer since the inception of televised media. A man whose power in 'the business' made *The Last Tycoon* look like Mickey Mouse.

CHAPTER II

SAN IGNACIO, BELIZE

In 1980, I left my home town of San Ignacio in the province of Cayo, Belize, and my five-year-old daughter, to find work in the United States. Like so many Belizeanas, I am a single mother. Fate gifted me a beautiful, crippled child, born with fire in her blood; I needed the money to pay for her medical care. My family fed, clothed, watched after her – there is only room for love in the *palapa* huts of the poor. Esmé arrived with straight tawny hair like her father's, but with my green cat's eyes, and coffee colored skin. She is quick to anger, quicker to laugh.

I was born Nelia Villa Lobos in Belize at a time it was known as British Honduras, and then regarded as a 'crown colony'. Britain finally saw fit to give us freedom in 1973, the year I turned thirteen. I know this much for sure because I have not only studied the birth records, but our own short history as a country. But understanding the legend of how my Pancho Villa forbears found themselves in Honduras is like trying to trace mangrove roots in a fog. As a poet wrote about me long afterwards:

> *Nelia hailed from the rural state of Cayo,*
> *her wits her only wealth,*
> *save some mangoes growing in the Bayou.*
> *(Note how the poet 'Cayo' and 'bayou'*
> *subtly blends, perverting horticultural laws*
> *to meet his ends)*

Of course, there are no bayous in Cayo, but a sluggish tropical stream, the *Rio Macal*, which bisects my hometown, San Ignacio. We owed our livelihood to its brown water, because unlike the farmers and ranchers resident in our village, my Papa was a *pescador:* an occupation less profitable than tending herds of goats, chickens, pigs, or raising armies of gibnuts or *pacas,* rat-like creatures, which ended up skewered and fried. We were tenants on a mango plantation. My forebears were 'landed' only in the sense that they had somehow washed up on the shores of Belize, or migrated through the jungles of the Yucatan looking for work or food. Who knows?

As a child lying on my back in the tall pampas grass, I recalled the rumors where my ancestors *might* be from. I imagined my great grandfather Pancho Villa breaking through the clouds on *Siete Leguas,* his stallion, galloping to the rescue of Mexican liberty. Mama claimed *her* grandmother was Valentina Ramirez Avitia, the famous *revolutionaria* 'La Valentina' of song and legend. Others, however, whispered she was just a consequence of Villa's rape of La Valentina's mother, Petra Espinosa of Parral, herself the offspring of incest with Pancho's sister, Mariana. Perhaps La Valentina was conceived by one of his many counterfeit wives, who can say? When I stared at the reflection of my green eyes in the Macal, I believed them to be the eyes of Valentina, though the only surviving pictures of her are painted in song and story. Are not those often the most accurate?

Though I was told photos of Francisco Villa and his 'true' wife, Dona Luz Corral de Villa, exist in museums, the images of his 'other' women have not survived. I marveled at the story told about Villa before he got to my great grandmother: he whipped to death a rival suitor with a bull's penis, a *bastinado.*[1] Had he sliced it from a living bull, or bought it, cured, in a *mercado*? What was fact, what was

---

[1] Ambrose Bierce, who was a Peregrine, defined '*bastinado*' as 'the act of walking on wood without exertion'.
~ *The Devil's Dictionary,* Ambrose Bierce, Wordsworth Editions Ltd.

fantasy? He certainly pursued women in romantic, bloody ways. As I grew older, I sensed the unusual heat in my own blood. There was little use bragging of absent ancestors to the frightened, tattered children of San Ignacio, creole descendants of slaves. They knew nothing of Pancho Villa. I must have seemed a giantess to them, and they avoided me.

Looking back, what Mama deplored as my willfulness but I called bravery, enriched my family in unexpected ways.

My Papa was a simple man who ate morsels of rice and vegetables which could not nourish a locust; he invented and made for me simple toys from garbage: a bamboo flute, a triangular boomerang of woven popsicle sticks, which if thrown correctly, returned, but otherwise flew into pieces on impact. I learned to reweave them so they flew again.

My Mother, from whom I get my height, towered over Papa and stoned him mercilessly with rubble from her own world of pain. She did not spare me the occasional blow during her little *chubascos,* or fits.

I watched and learned as Papa baited trotlines with fresh water clams to tempt blue catfish onto his hooks. The small *bilam,* sacred to the Maya, could be netted, but didn't make much of a meal. And there was many a day that our small *pescaderia* had only frozen *camarones* to sell, trucked sixty-five miles from the coastline. Don't you consider the business of bait, hook, and line complex, unsporting, and chancy? I did. So one day, I whittled a triple spear of ash modeled on a drawing of one carried by a bloke in a picture book, dived from a large rock into a hole, touched bottom some two fathoms below, and swam upriver until I came upon a blue catfish motionless in the lazy current. I killed him with a single stab behind the gills. I rarely missed.

I learned to keep hungry bottom feeders in place by suspending a stocking full of freshwater clams from an overhanging branch, and then taught myself how to hold my breath and stroke against the current upriver to surprise quarries. While the golden scaled *bilam* fade quickly into eternal darkness once exposed to the sun, catfish take asphyxiation in stride and have to be whacked in the head with a cosh, or they will try to slide off the bank and twist back into the river. Some of these catfish were half my weight, but I wrestled them ashore.

I swatted at the schools of piranha, less aggressive than their Amazon cousins, which found parts of me appetizing. I became very fit. I imagined my flaring hips, wasp waist, and taut breasts as those of my ancestress. Like the river my body began to ebb and flow; I kept my tides in check with wads of Kleenex.

There were other slimy predators. The local parish priest pretended to find me disrespectful and took pains to dandle me on his knee and talk in circles about the devil, temptations of the flesh, St. Theresa and the Romans, and my too tight fitting linen shift. Once while pretending to chastise or bless me he touched my breasts so I elbowed him in the *cojones* and put an end to all that. None of the villagers, and certainly, not the priest, would have been strong enough to hold me down for any purpose. Though I attended the old mission school, I developed a reputation of a wildcat. I played soccer. I considered the Catechism *basura* and confessionals as outhouses for the weak. I loved Cervantes, *The Adventures of Huckleberry Finn*, and *Winnie the Pooh,* a biography of Churchill, a biography of Gandhi. Hemingway's *The Old Man and the Sea* became a particular favorite. Ferocious purple fish flared from its faded dun and ebony pages.

These books, and others, were given to me in exchange for babysitting, by an American hippy family touring Belize one summer. They carried Baltimore Catechisms, which became tinder to start our stove. After reading Steinbeck's *Journal of the Sea of Cortez,* I longed to meet the sea creatures described therein, whose cousins waited off the coast of Belize. After reading *The Grapes of Wrath,* my social sentiments became more radical than Marx. I began to keep my own journal which I hid in the roots of a mango tree.

When I turned sixteen, I was allowed to accompany Papa on trips to Belize City, in the family's old '37 Ford pickup, its sides mottled like a grouper by patches of primer and rust – *La Cabrilla.* We used it to haul shrimp and ice from the coast. Papa is a little guy, five feet tall and no more than 120 pounds, and by then I was, what, six foot one? We made an odd pair. Not long thereafter, I found an old mask and snorkel washed up on the beach, and used them to dive below a dock by the old swing bridge, searching for crayfish. We expanded our menu at the *pescaderia.* By this time, I needed that old black bikini top I found discarded on the tourist beach. Whatever was hidden beneath my light shifts of cotton or linen continued to tempt the priest. I could see it in his anemone eyes.

"Dios mío," exclaimed a wrinkled fisherman sitting on the dock, "that dress swirls around your legs like cream in *café leche.* Isn't it . . . inconvenient?" But Papa insisted on the modesty it conferred.

When the launch from Ambergris Key unloaded groups of sunburned tourists dockside, I stared with fascination from beneath the pier planks, my curly hair floating behind my mask as I scanned the undersides of the departing guests. The color and diversity of the women's bikini bottoms or panties startled me: there were no birds in Cayo with plumage quite like that.

Once, when the launch's propeller became fouled in a net, the gringo skipper tossed me a knife, asked me to dive below and cut away the snarl. I finished this work rapidly. When he handed me a few coins, I followed his eyes scanning my body: "I finally understand why the ancient seafarers spun legends about mermaids," he said. He claimed it was my eyes he particularly noted, "panther like, their lights enhanced by the noonday sun glancing off ripples in the water." Then my outstretched hand reached forward to grasp the coins.

The skipper asked whether I had come to Belize City by myself, if I had companions, and I pointed to Papa, who impatiently gunned the clattering motor of *La Cabrilla*. Departing fishermen pack their plunder of permit and wahoo in dry iced Styrofoam. One had been left on board by mistake. The skipper gave it to my Papa in further payment for my services; he later admitted he sought favor with Papa because "we are happy to employ girls like you on the island." But he was too shrewd to show bad form by proposing anything during this first meeting. In conversation with Papa, he learned we came from San Ignacio once a week on Thursdays to retrieve iced *camarones*, and he arranged to be on hand the following week, dockside, when we appeared.

My employment was then discussed with Papa as though I were absent. I would reside on the island and have Sundays off. If the launch happened to return early that day, I could take the bus to visit my family. The dismal joys of Belize City would be no lure: I would be island-bound on my day off, available for work. My duties would include assisting instructors on the dive boat, filling oxygen tanks, unpeeling wetsuits in the day, and at night, working the bar.

The prospects of diving off Ambergris Caye, a place visited only in my dreams, excited me; its reefs held some of the most unusual sea creatures on the planet, lurking in the fabled 'Blue Hole'. The promised wages tempted Papa. They were ten times more than he could earn from the *pescaderia*. In any event, by this time I was full tired of spearing and clubbing catfish. The skipper described Caya Esmeralda as an exclusive resort for *Norte Americanos*; generous tips could be expected in addition to the pay. I could keep those, Papa said. The resort provided housing, meals, 'uniforms' for the bar, and all dive equipment. Its management transformed us with exotic creole names. My badge would identify me as Desireé, unless I chose a different name, but it had to be French. "Why?" Papa wanted to know. "To protect the privacy of our guests and our employees," said the skipper. We had no idea what he meant. My Spanish name reminded me of a *vaca* I had read about in a golden book; I was more than glad to be done with it. Desireé would suit me fine. I knew what it meant. The skipper said he would return for me in a week. My mother settled matters at the mission school. I could, of course, bring books with me, maintain my studies, and use the library at the resort to further my education.

CHAPTER III

CAYA ESMERALDA

The following week, after the boat collected me and my mesh bag of humble belongings, its engines soon reached speed, knifing through the cobalt blue waters of San Pedro Bay. The engines sang of a new beginning, and I was happy for that. On the cusp of an exciting adventure, all one's senses come alive. As the sea spray lashed my face, this is what I saw: flying fish dancing off the front of the boat in white spray, an ocean camouflaged by shades of white, turquoise, and deep cobalt blue, as dappled green canopies concealed the jungle.

Fringes of palm trees decorated the horizon like candles on a birthday cake. I asked what 'ambergris' meant; the skipper gave me a strange look and said he didn't know; but afterwards, I found it in a dictionary in the library, which revealed: 'ambergris is a biliary secretion of the intestines of the sperm whale.' Literally, whale shit. It must be something like that pink glue Mama gave us when we had croup; because the hard beaks of giant squid, a favorite food of the sperm whale, were once found embedded in ambergris clumps washed up on the translucent sands of the cayes. But when I approached Ambergris Caye for the first time, no whale breached to greet us, nor, as I discovered later, did whale shit pepper the sands. Perhaps the whales had all run away by then.

As the craft swung northward, past the small town of San Pedro, Caya Esmeralda appeared on the western tip of Ambergris Caye.

The skipper, during his courting of Papa, described Caya Esmeralda as one of the most expensive resorts in the world. Guests arrived by boat, seaplane, luxury yacht, or helicopter.

The small caye embraced five guesthouses, which reminded me, as the launch approached, of shimmering pyramids I saw in an Egyptian travelogue. Metallic sunbeams bounced off their white triangular roofs like notes from a steel band. You could almost hear them whisper their names as they shimmered in the heat: Magnolia, Hibiscus, Bougainvillea, the circumference of the blossom reflective of the suite's luxury.

On the western side of the resort, away from the restaurant, dive shop, pool bar, and guesthouses, camouflaged by hedges of sea grape, were employee housing and canteen, along with several elevated open-air *palapa* huts with hammocks. These digs did not differ from those at home, except I would have three Creole roommates: a bar girl and two kitchen helpers. Slutty, heavy breasted, dull-eyed creatures, much shorter than me, they laughed easily, and when they saw me coming yelled "*wadge ou fo dehn janny fiddler.*" I spoke Kriol, or Gullah, fairly good Spanish, and, as you must know by now, even better English. With their heavy West Indies accent, I had problems interpreting some of the slang of my *palapa* mates.

The other difference between this kip and Cayo was, land crabs with stalked eyes infested this Cayo. Each had its own personality, seemingly unafraid, and bold as brass. No sooner had I dropped my mesh bag on the raised plank flooring of the hut than two of these flamingo coloured pirates began dragging it away. How had they gotten in the hut? Could they climb the rope ladders, which led to the elevated sleeping platform? I would have to fetch an ab iron. In fact, these clever blokes scaled the sloping palm trees with ease, then dropped from their fronds to the thatched roof, burrowed through it to the lodge poles, and scampered to the floor. I thought whacking one and leaving its carcass on the floor might put them off, but they just dragged it off and ate it.

The guests came in three varieties: young wealthy

newlyweds on honeymoon, who stayed in their suites making love or fighting; groups of business executives with contracted *novias*, who wanted to dive, drink, fish and party hard; and wealthy elders who paddled around the reef for a morning snorkel, and in the afternoon read novels by Graham Greene, beneath white cabanas to escape the broiling sun. I avidly read the titles hoping they might leave their books behind. Sometimes I would see works by the American author named Phillip Roth in their hands. The library had a full collection of his writing, and I came to learn what white people, at least, certain white people, do to each other. The island was also a time-out box for what the management called 'cybercoolies'; burnt out technicians from the second wave of the information revolution; no computers, cellphones, or other gadgets were allowed these refugees on the island. They always appeared to me as a little lost.

These waters were alive with rays, hawksbill, and the occasional lumberjack sea turtle (endangered – during that time it was believed only *certain* of God's creations had become 'endangered'.) Nurse and reef sharks, and tiaras of tropical fish crowned coral heads, including trigger, tang, clown, parrot, and angelfish.

I enjoyed filling oxygen tanks, washing and checking dive suits, masks, snorkels, regulators, other scuba associated truck, and, after helping guests suit up, tutoring them in the dangers and delights of the coral chasms of the cayes. I did not relish peeling the suits off their pekid bodies, which reminded me of skinning catfish.

I thought about cutting my hair for convenience, but exposure to saltwater and sun gave it some deep red highlights I thought attractive, so I let it spill to my waist.

I did not look forward to the nighttime work as a bartender, but learned to concoct the treacled toxins tourists in tropical climes think they should consume: margaritas, piña coladas, mai tais, zombies, and the occasional cosmopolitan, then coming into style. Bilikin, the local hearty beer, flowed freely, and imported kegs of Guinness caused disputes among the guests. One would argue it could not travel without being destroyed; another claimed the best Guinness was served on an island off Ireland. Though its popularity started with London dockhands, it now seemed to be the beverage of the wealthy. None of this affected me since I don't take alcohol. I ate my usual fish, fruit, and rice, or *bam bam*, a home-style dish made with cassava. I made notes in my journal and increased my vocabulary.

Time flew by on Caya Esmeralda. I conducted myself as a professional, and the guests were usually polite. Males flirted with me from time to time; even the odd female butterfly brushed me with her wings, but never left any dust. Had this occurred, no law would chain me, though in Belize City such money making conduct was encouraged. I did notice that, when all-male executive groups came to the island, on their third or fourth night one or more of my roommates went missing. I could tell by their street clothes and the cheap jewelry they occasionally wore (the employee uniforms were white shorts, polo shirts, and pith helmets for the men; shorts and black halter-tops for the women) that they must be cocking a snoot.

Then, two weeks before Christmas, a group of five *jim jam* white guys checked into the resort. Each occupied his own bungalow, which usually slept four. Word had it they arrived in a private jet at Belize airport: fly fishermen engaged in a global competition to catch the largest bonefish. I had never seen a bonefish, and from the rude jokes made about them, I first concluded that they were mythical. But the boat boys said they could be caught at certain times on the coral heads.

I later learned there were larger stakes at risk. I made notes in my journal of the strange, sometimes whispered conversations of these men at the bar. Before Ambergris, they had fished Islamorada in the Florida Keys; been skunked at Andros in the Bahamas; had visited the coral reefs of remote Christmas Island; and after jetting all the way back to Caya Esmeralda to try their luck, they would make a final stop in Molokai, where there were reputed to be the ghosts of lepers onshore, and off the reefs, *oi'o,* the largest bonefish in the world.

One of the guests, by his looks the youngest, did not accompany his fellows on the dive boat or fishing launch, spending much of his day doing laps in the pool, or lying about, consuming books with names I could not decipher, from a respectful distance. From time to time, he would scribble like a mad thing on a yellow pad, sometimes gazing with pleasure at what he had written, more often, crumpling the sheet in disgust.

Staff were not supposed to make direct eye contact with the guests; I took the measure of this man, as well as his companions. I later learned twin brothers, heirs to an Alabaman lumber fortune, owned the jet, and had brought along their banker, insurance broker, and doctor. The reader-writer was their self-described 'fifth wheel', whatever that meant. When he appeared, alone, in the bar at cocktail hour, on an evening where the setting sun flared like an open wound, my curiosity got the better of me and I flashed him a couple of looks. A man who found books more compelling than scuba diving or fishing might justify a scrimmage.

He politely ordered, in the manner of one accustomed to such luxuries, a Pimm's Cup Number 3, a drink left over from our British occupation. I quickly learned the recipe from my bartender's guide. It was simple: syrup from a Pimm's Cup bottle and ginger beer. Sipping on it slowly, he asked my name, inquired whether I enjoyed reading, what 'rowed my boat', and rewarded my answers with a recitation of a poem about a bunny and a 'prophylactic pup', throughout which he looked directly into my eyes without staring at my breasts, which relaxed me.

When I mistakenly asked his name, he replied, sardonically, "The inevitable hooker."

"Nice to meet you, Señor Inevitable," I said, having no idea what the devil he might mean.

I thought his name must have something to do with bonefishing, but recalled, too late, that guests' names were supposed to be anonymous to the staff; we were instructed to address them as 'Sir' or 'Madame'. Maybe he was just keeping me away from that trouble.

I learned, much later, that he was a lawyer for the brothers, a bagman earning ten percent of whatever cash he could smuggle through customs for deposit in offshore banks. He later told me it was more honest than sweating over time sheets, billing clients in tenths of hours for illusions, and easier than grinding out false invoices. The brothers, protected by some legal privilege or other, and by the pretense of a bonefishing contest, could deny knowledge of the smuggled cash; 'Sr. Inevitable' filed no forms implicating them. He later told me he became famous for taking big risks for appropriate fees.

As the sun dived beneath the horizon, no doubt embarrassed by what was to unfold that night, billionaire brother *numero dos*, who fished the flats all day every day, struggled up from the beach, pulled out the stool next to 'Sr. Inevitable', and mumbled, as if to no one: "Fucking bonefish. Fucking boneheaded bonefish."

He had the craggy build of a breakwater, straight, salt and pepper hair swept back over a sunburned forehead. His ground beefsteak face, otherwise handsome, perched on a sliced Bermuda onion neck. He was streaked with salt like an empty margarita glass. It was the kind of look that might inspire a middle-aged blond-tinted American woman to take a bite of him, as if he were steak tartar. I borrow this image from a short story I once read by the bloke Hemingway. He had been drinking heavily on the boat back.

"Fuck me. Fuck me in the ass," he grumbled, regarding me with a vacant glance because his bleary eyes had not yet adjusted to the darkness of the bar.

"Give me a Bilister and a double demerara back," he finally barked.

"Bad day on the flats?" crooned 'Sr. Inevitable'. He used his best silver-edged voice like on an old Bing Crosby record.

"I tell you: broke off half a dozen ghost shrimp flies in as many hours. The sons of bitching bones take off like locomotives. If you try to restrain 'em, they snap the leader; if you let 'em run, they're over the falls, abrade the tippet on the coral, end of discussion. And the guides are not worth the powder to blow 'em to hell. Not worth the powder to blow 'em to hell."

"Harrison is forced to use tippets like cobwebs," politely explained 'Sr. Inevitable'.

I hadn't a clue what he meant. Harrison Scott looked from 'Sr. Inevitable' to me and back again as if we were co-conspirators. Then he shook his head in despair, lamenting his fate in a rolling Southern accent, which somehow reminded me of Huck's raft cruising down the Mississippi. I placed a sweating Bilister in front of him, and splashed a generous dram of golden spirits into a crystal snifter from a dark brown bottle of Lemon Hart. He regarded it with suspicion.

Without looking at the bottle, he snarled: "That ain't *demerara* rum, sweetheart, that's *Lemming Head* Barbados rum. Fetch me up some *demerara* rum, now, like a good girl."

"Excuse me sir, this *is* demerara rum!" I said, politely.

"Bullshit." He took a swig of the Bilister and knocked back the glass of rum.

"Hmmm," he said, "there sure is only one way to tell." And he grabbed the bottle, spilled a dollop onto the highly polished teak bar, struck a match, and dropped it in the puddle. '*Whoooooooooooooosh*', went the mixture, slightly scorching the faces of both men, almost knocking them from their bar stools.

"See?" snarled Harrison Scott, "if that was *real* demerara branded rum, it wouldn't have backfired like cheap gasoline, it'd burn slow, smooth, real pretty, like this black bitch tryin' to put one over on us. At the rate I'm paying for this fuckin' sand spit, ya'd think they would have premium grade rum on board."

"Go easy on the poor girl, Harrison; *demerara* isn't a *brand* of rum, it's a *type* of rum. Read the goddamned bottle!"

"Fuck you, counselor. Fuck you all to hell. Or, haven't you heard? The client is always right."

As I leaned over the bar, rag in hand, attempting to swab the scar of soot from its polished surface, Scott pinched my nipple between his thumb and index finger and said, "Come on honey, let's do *bam bam* in the cabana, you can make it up to me."

I yelped in pain, instinctively reached for the neck of the half-empty bottle of Bilister to brain him with it. But 'Sr. Inevitable' had already unleashed a roundhouse right which caught Scott upside the head and knocked him from the bar stool onto the ground.

Scott, his brother, and the others departed the hotel early the next morning without their 'fifth wheel', not because they were bored with the fishing, but because Scott needed medical attention not readily available either on Ambergris

Caye or Belize City. That left my savior without a ride back to San Francisco, from a now relatively abandoned Esmeralda Caye.

I don't know whether he dropped his yellow lined pad behind the bar intentionally after the skirmish. But while Scott lay passed out on the floor, the lawyer had scribbled on the front page: 'Call the White Witch . . . return Scott files to general counsel . . . Montgomery . . . pre-empt nasty letters . . . tender assault and battery claim to insurance company . . . State Bar problem? Probably not . . . cash is king. Time will tell.'

My gossipy roommates came up with all kinds of improbable reasons why these guests departed early; I had been instructed by our manager to say nothing.

I kept Sr. Inevitable's yellow pad, hoping he would find me and ask for it. Though I felt sorry he had been left behind because of his gallantry, I secretly rejoiced in the fact that we might share the same remote sliver of earth for a few more days. The next afternoon, with no duties at either the dive shop or boat, I prepared, in the now deserted bar, a well-iced Pimm's Cup #3 and carried it and the legal pad to poolside, on a tray without a chit.

"On the house," I smiled.

He gazed at me over a thick volume, *The Gathering Storm,* by Winston S. Churchill.

"I must apologize for my friend," he said, "but thank you for the drink. Thank you for my pad!"

"What is that one about?" I asked, pointing to the book.

"Oh, about a man who liked black swans, painting, new bricks, old brandy, and single-handedly inspired others to save Western civilization."

"About a hero man, like you!"

"Would you like a book to read?" he gestured toward stack of both hard and paperbacks, some new, some well worn, by his side. "What kind of story might interest you?"

"One filled with passion, deep sea creatures, and watercress sandwiches." For the first time, he smiled.

"Somehow I don't think Hemingway or Verne ate tea sandwiches. Well, there are *some* short stories in this book which come close."

And he handed me two books, the first *Nine Stories* by J.D. Salinger.

"They are a little . . . Zionist. But you needn't worry about that. If you finish all those tonight, tomorrow there will be a test – and a prize!"

"My thanks. What strange names!" I marveled glancing at the titles, as I slowly walked away. I made sure to move so that he carefully followed me with his eyes. We will save a detailed description of his appearance for later. I will never forget it, because the second book he gave me was called *Tender is the Night* by a bloke named F. Scott Fitzgerald.

That night, in the unlit sleeping verandah, with the help of a torch, I devoured the short stories. I looked up the word 'Zionist'. Later, he told me that all Jewish writing is a little Zionist. That they can't help it. Or don't want to help it. Or something.

For once, I was not distracted by the snorts and gurgles of sleeping roommates nor the clicking and scratching of foraging land crabs. I found but one sea creature in the book, a banana fish. And the bloke in the story used it as bait to hit on a little girl. Oh, there was another story about a dinghy, sure enough, which featured goggles, but the little boy in that story threw them in the water. What a spoiled brat, I thought. I confess that when reading about when the banana fish man kissed the instep of the little girl, parts of me tingled. Why had I been given this book? Why had *he* given me this book? I combed its pages for a watercress sandwich. No such luck.

The story's end reminded me of *un Viejo* who once came to the island. His younger wife attended the dive boat each day, darting hungry looks at the biceps of the bucks manhandling the heavy oxygen tanks. The maids said the poor bloke waited for her return in their room playing videos of trains: steam trains, passenger trains, freight trains, trains with cowcatcher fronts, coal filled tenders, and cabooses. And solitaire – the first time I heard about such a card game. The videos showed locomotives bullying their way along tracks somewhere in the American south, smokestacks belching ash and cinders. Though the temperature on Caya Esmeralda rarely falls below 75°, he also watched, over and over, a video of blazing, cheery logs, tears streaming down his face. And this is what was playing when the maid found him, dressed in blue deck shoes, tan slacks, and a woolen shirt of green and black plaid like those skirts Scottish bagpipers wear: dead from an overdose of a drug called Nembutal.

The next afternoon, thinking of suicides and the whys of them, I prepared, not another Pimm's Cup, but a banana daiquiri, intending to use it as an opening to discuss the short story. Clever, no? *Christo* was I dumb. Curious to learn more about my benefactor, I peered at him through the tropical foliage while he scribbled away beneath his cabana. How he appeared is etched in more than my memory: it was the eyes. The eyes had it. They blazed from a face partially concealed by a thatch of wheaten hair worn like a fare-thee-well over a high forehead. Those eyes could kill, chill, cool, or fool. They were designed for all occasions, shaded blue, grey, turquoise, or bottle-green, depending upon light or mood.

"What's this?" he exclaimed, as I quickly set down the drink and turned away. "Come, now . . . Mademoiselle *De-si-reé*," glancing at my badge, "you are going to get fired giving me free drinks."

He was the type of man who would have slit his own throat before showing intellectual weakness by improperly pronouncing a foreign name. He articulated my name as though he were about to pounce on it.

"If I were going to be fired," I said, "I would have been put off the island yesterday. Ready for my test!" I said, rolling the 'rs' in the Spanish way and showing him a bit of tongue. He later told me my rolling 'rs' reminded him of incoming waves.

"I don't administer exams in the glare of the noonday sun," he said, seeding a cloud of disappointment. So I again turned away.

"But I'll tell you what; when do you get off?"

I hesitated, and murmured, without facing him, "The bar closes at midnight."

"Well, I am sure there is a rule here that staff cannot join guests in their rooms. But guess what? There are now four *empty* suites on this island, and we can meet in one after hours. It will be an open book exam. Multiple choice, no trick questions."

I considered this, and turned around. He dangled a key from a magnolia blossom cast in brass, which glittered in the sunlight. He must have snagged this from reception where they hang on a mahogany board. What gumption! He had planned this out! Had I been that obvious?

"If I can, it will have to be after my roommates fall asleep."

"I will make it worth your while."

What could he mean by this? Did he take me for a *puta*? I gave him benefit of the doubt. I slipped away, wondering, like all girls facing such adventures, what to wear. It would have to be something black, something that would help me slip, undetected, through the night.

Before sleeping, I turned over the back of the second book, the one by Fitzgerald. It showed a picture of him. And he was a dead ringer for Sr. Inevitable.

CHAPTER IV

IN THE HILLS OF BEVERLY II

When I boarded the airplane, I had a chance to open and read the contents of the envelope marked:

"SHANE FITZGERALD, ESQ.
ATTORNEY CLIENT PRIVILEGED AND
CONFIDENTIAL"

It warned against comments about Mrs. Golden's five million dollar diamond belt buckle, which she was sure to wear to the meeting.

Instructed me to avoid discussions about money or fees. "Those would be taken care of." Cautioned me not to comment on the fact that, last holiday season, she imported dump trucks of snow to the semi-tropical Hills of Beverly to give the children a 'White Christmas.'

Prohibited questions asking whether exotic seashells had been planted on the strand in front of the Goldens' palatial Malibu bide-a-wee, so their two children could easily find them on their walks.

Or if this beach house was kept fully staffed and provisioned should the Reagans, en route to Rancho del Cielo, wish to spend a few days at the beach.

Oh, and the patrol car with dummies in the cops' uniforms parked in front of the mansion? I was not to be troubled about that; it was only a prop from one of Andrew Golden's prime time TV shows, on display to dissuade evil circus wizards.

When Winsome 'Collie' Green, then the most powerful Democrat in Sacramento, phoned my office to say 'a Beverly Hills bagman and fixer' would be calling with an urgent other cautions were given, intended to keep the flow of political donations coming his way. But those orders, by an unidentified author, were over the top.

This boy Collie had come a long way from his provenance as the son of black sharecroppers in Texas to graduating from Hastings College of the Law; from representing pimps and prostitutes to becoming speaker of the Assembly of the Late Great State of California. Collie's connection with Mr. Golden was indirect but profound.

Golden was the son of an impoverished tailor in Dallas, Texas. Though Collie had been sure to chuck his Southern accent, Mr. Golden still had a wisp of it. They were both getting their own back at the power structure that had bowed their ancestors: Golden, by satirizing the foibles of Texas oilmen and their women in one of his serials, Collie by smiting oil interests whenever he got the chance as Speaker of the California Assembly.

I felt it prudent to inquire: "Why aren't these famous folks using their high-priced Beverly Hills counsel?"

"Why refer this to San Francisco counsel?" Collie asked. "Because, one, this is a highly sensitive matter and Beverly Hills is a small town peopled by big mouths; and two, Ratatt, Flisk *et al*, the Goldens' usual counsel, have thrown up their hands. Told them there's nothing to be done. When you are given all the facts, you will see what I mean."

"If 240 hack-in-the-box Demo power broker lawyers can't help 'em, what the hell am I supposed to do?"

"C'mon, Fitzgerald, you are the mouthpiece of the hopeless and the damned! This is right up your alley: a beautiful escaped felon, a comatose child, clients who don't care how much you charge as long as the job gets done."

"Right. Which means, if I take the case, I can't afford to lose it. Because if I do, *you* lose one of your cash cows."

"Oh, I wouldn't refer the case if I thought for a moment you were going to *lose* it, bad boy! And, Shane, there is an added bonus – trains! You love trains."

"Trains, as in what brides pull after them? They scare me."

"No. Trains, as in *The California Zephyr*."

"Lions, and tigers and bears, oh my!"

"Right. Check in later. After you get the call."

Not five minutes elapsed before 'the fixer' came on the line. I made him wait the requisite ninety seconds before picking up. Never show anxiety. Rich, powerful people are festooned with functionaries. Nothing has changed since the days of The Sun King. Neanderthal chieftains probably threw beaters in front of saber-toothed tigers before casting the first spear.

'The fixer' proved to be a thoroughly nasty little bastard. Though I did not know it at the time, his home, within walking distance of the mansion of his prospective clients, was guarded by killer carp. Yes, killer carp, distant relatives of the geese Lord Byron kept beneath the floorboards of his coach to deter bandits. The entrance to *chez fixer* could only be reached by crossing a walled courtyard, which concealed a deep, ebony pool. Uncemented flagstones in a jigsaw pattern rested on pilasters of steel rising vertically from the bottom of the pond.

It pleased 'the fixer' to observe prospective guests teeter their way between crevasses which initially appeared as black enameled grout between these stepping stones – their edges were in fact ankle-catching, razor-sharp escarpments. A visitor's trek became all the more challenging by the shade cast from overhanging *gunnera* plants, with giant leaves which not only eclipsed the light but presented additional obstacles to safe passage. The carp floated below like orange, pink, and white balloons, smacking their gummy lips. The most one could lose would be a foot.

During his first telephone call, 'the fixer's' primary concern was negotiating a suitable referral fee. I coldly informed him that the law offices of Shane Fitzgerald did not pay referral fees, and, in any event, it would be unethical to establish one in advance of understanding the complexities of the assignment.

'The fixer' countered that a percentage of fees billed would be expected, and that they could be paid to Collard's mistress, in cash, at her ebony-and-ivory upholstered Pacific Heights lair; to which I rejoined that 'the fixer' and Collard should be more concerned with the likelihood of success, given what I understood to be the urgency of the mission. I was assured enough jack flew between the Hills of Beverly and Pacific Heights to pad the fees. The clients didn't care.

A recent survey of the American people disclosed that 78% believed lawyers to be dishonest. So my recitation of the various ethical problems created by referral fees was not intended to deter 'the fixer' from the chase; to the contrary, 'the fixer' might have thrown this out as a red herring to ferret out dishonesty. At least, he was being forced to report my probity. In fact, I could give a good goddamn about propriety – I needed the money, and would pad my fees with the amount necessary to get it, even if I had to pay it in bananas to chimpanzees.

'The fixer' arranged an after-hours dinner meeting with the Goldens. My Cessna 410 would be flown into Santa Monica Airport. I was careful to tell 'the fixer' about my private plane with private pilot and little wine bar aboard. This marketing tool created the impression that if not a prominent lawyer, at least I was an expensive one. Of course a professional pilot would captain the plane; I could hardly drive a car, let alone twist little radio dials while wrestling with a joystick.

During the late afternoon flight from Concord-Buchanan airport in the East Bay, a jet stream of 110 knots whipped the Cessna along so that the 365 miles between airports took less than 45 minutes, and also rinsed the LA basin of smog. That produced one of those crisp, cloudless, California late winter days. The sun disappearing behind Santa Barbara Island looked like an angry bruise, when it should have reminded me of a pot of gold.

I thought of myself then as a highly intuitive man. It dawned on me that this might be a dangerous assignment. Maybe the Los Angeleno lawyers had shied away because the case was too risky; and cases which on their face looked too good to be true always came with the proverbial woodpile nigger: they were either personally dangerous, or the lawyer was expected to do something that could get him disbarred. I sorted these unwelcome thoughts in my noggin as the plane touched down at Santa Monica Municipal airport one half hour ahead of schedule.

Two white limousines waited end to end within the barbed wire confines of the airport. This was at a time before the nation's airports had been converted into armed camps; a time when one could hop aboard a Pacific Southwest Airlines jet and buy a ticket on board, get two free drink tickets from a coy, hot-panted stewardess and maybe a roll in the hay with her that evening; a time during the golden age of age discrimination, when warty old heifers tossing little bags of peanuts at the compressed passengers were not permitted on commercial aircraft.

The tower instructed the pilot to bring the plane to rest alongside the limos. As the props whined to a standstill the uniformed driver of the second limousine opened its rear door, and a small, wiry figure emerged. Andrew Golden was adorned in black: some sort of nylon windbreaker of the type used by baseball managers when they walk to the mound to change pitchers, over well-tailored gabardine slacks, ending in small feet embraced by black velvet Shipton and Heneage slippers with gilded crests depicting crossed golf clubs, polo mallets, or cudgels monogrammed on their toes. For the most part, Winston Churchill ran World War II while wearing a pair.

While inept at corralling details in litigation, I then thought myself a master at observing them. And the trivia of which I was not aware would only fill a small notebook. So the fact that Golden wore slippers *and was smoking a pipe* stirred some excitement, as though the solution to *The Mystery of the Speckled Band* was about to be revealed.

Golden, like an emperor about to pass judgment on a gladiator, inclined his head of close cropped silver hair, reached for my briefcase, handed it to the driver, looked up, and fixing me with his large, brown, doe-like eyes softly said: "So you are Collie's guy. They say you are capable of anything. We have a big problem down here. Welcome."

Golden gestured at the seat opposite him in the limousine. I not only associated the sweet smell of pipe smoke in the limo with Sherlock Holmes, but with my deceased father and his silver tins of Four Square tobacco.

"I hope you don't mind my pipe," said Golden, "happy to knock out the ashes, but it's soothing when editing these damn rushes." He clearly assumed I knew the meaning of this technical term. I had no idea. Visions of baby Moses concealed by reeds flashed before my eyes. The limousine featured a small conversation pit with juxtaposed benches fitted with video monitors.

"We'll meet Mandy at La Scala and we'll go over the whole *mishigas* with you. But while we're driving, if you don't mind, I'll finish these rushes. Seven hours of prime time television means I've got to work while driving." He had a soft southern accent. Where had he acquired *that*?

Aha! Rushes must be his unedited sitcoms.

"Never mind at all, do the rushes, however Biblical; do the pipe, it reminds me of Sherlock Holmes and my Dad."

Golden regarded me with a doubtful look.

One monitor displayed *The Sub Tub,* a sitcom featuring the adventures of a daft crew, which had run their submarine aground on a tropical island during World War II. The other simultaneously ran an episode of *Nepotism*, a more caustic soap about a despotic millionaire who appoints eight offspring by four different wives to various positions in his business empire, and referees their consequent knife fights, ill-concealed as domestic struggles for Daddy's attention. I focused on Joan Collins' boobs, an uplifting sight that could indeed give males a rush.

Golden would pivot between benches so he could view each program, clutching a hand-held remote by which he edited scenes. He observed me staring at one of the screens.

"Oh, don't focus on the rushes if you don't mind," Golden said firmly, but not unkindly, "until we get to know you better."

So I stared out the window. I couldn't help reading the signs:

"God Bless America – Every Box On Sale!"

"Take Charge or Be Large." On a billboard for diet supplements.

"Chronic Tacos."

"Thai One On."

"Undo Tattoos."

"Shear Confessions." A hairdressing salon moniker.

"Legal Grounds." At a coffee stand near a courthouse.

The limousine was slowing down. It crossed gently over

a yellow signed "Speed Hump." Post Victorian England does not name these fiendish thingies as such, but calls the process 'traffic calming.'

One couldn't resist glancing at the *Nepotism* screen to see what Joan Collins might be doing. All it displayed was John Forsythe's blue hair.

A billboard advertising divorce services extolled the virtues of "The Christian Lawyers." The last Christian died on the cross, I thought. I did not advertise. Didn't want the kinds of clients who bought products or services from billboards.

There were different joints advertising, "Nude," "Fat," and "Gross" burgers, respectively. But the topper – and had I known him better, Andrew Golden would have gotten a poke in the ribs so as to not miss this one – was a black woman on a street corner in shades, draped in green, like the Statue of Liberty, doing a braless hootchy-cootchy with a sign "Income Tax Services" hanging from her neck.

I didn't like paying taxes anyway, having been Berkeley indoctrinated in the avoidance of any war, like that in Vietnam, engineered to fatten the purses of the military industrial complex. Nor did I enjoy fattening booreaucraps of any stripe with what I conceived as my hard-earned money. I knew that Thomas Jefferson would eventually be proven right: thousands of them would have to be slapped upside a concrete wall and shot. It could come none too soon.

I suspected the flashcard images captured in the limo's passenger rear window had been selected for a reason: just couldn't work out their common denominator.

"It's just brain candy, spun to give the audience a sugar high, some respite from their humdrum lives," said Andrew Golden suddenly, as if to countermand his recent order. He hit the delete button on the remote. "You've got to cut away the crabgrass that strangles the magic."

A little research had uncovered Golden's m.o.: dredging up has-been actresses and actors from 60s, 70s, and even 50s television shows, still alive in the subconscious of audiences, to star in his productions; hawking nostalgia to gain market share. Old memories came cheap. So did these actors and actresses.

The limousines converged on the restaurant together. Golden popped the cassettes from the machines and handed them to his driver, who delivered them to a secretary in the first limousine. After it disgorged two rocky-looking customers in matching pearl gray suits with black ties, it sped off, presumably to the studio.

Inside the restaurant, opposing leather banquettes had been reserved for the Golden party, one, no doubt, for the heavies.

Presently, I observed a fit, middle-aged blond in a pink pantsuit sporting an Imelda Marcos coiffure with Debbie Reynolds bangs sweep, like the Empress of Siam, from yet a third white limousine, which appeared curbside. Bad idea to wear a five-million-dollar diamond belt buckle when meeting a lawyer to negotiate a fee, I mused. But I had been sworn to silence. My libido sprang to life, however, like tickertape on Black Friday. I rarely encountered a woman without imagining what she might be like in bed. I got on famously with women, in part, I believed, because at some level they must have known what I was thinking and appreciated the subconscious gesture. Since Mrs. Golden had the acquisitive aura of 'the fixer', she might be ferocious in the sack.

A tall stork of a man with thinning combed-back hair, wire-rimmed glasses, and a well-trimmed goatee followed her deferentially. In Egypt, he would have been the factotum bearing a large, peacock feathered fan. The shapes of his mouth and head recalled the existentialist sufferer of *The Scream*. From the gloom of the restaurant's entrails materialized the weasel face of 'the fixer'.

I found myself in the middle of the banquette wedged between the skinny existentialist and 'the fixer', with Andrew and Mandy Golden facing each other at either end. Mrs. Golden signified distress by twirling her empty long-stemmed wine glass. The existentialist and 'the fixer' exchanged feral glances familiar to all secret sharers. The bodyguards scowled from the opposite banquette, ready for wrongdoing. From a plan view, I realized the top of my head would appear as the center nail in one of opposing horseshoes.

It was only after the waiter formally presented menus that the shades lurking in other recesses of the bar crept forward.

'Collie' Green had been right: Beverly Hills is indeed a very small place. The information Golden would appear at La Scala that evening had been sold by the maitre d' to some service provider who spread the word to actors, actresses, film editors, cameramen, and others seeking work in an Andrew Golden sitcom or his production company.

Golden pretended to scan the menu for a brief moment, tossed it aside with a sigh, pecked at the rim of a glass of Evian water, and peered anxiously at his wife as she inhaled a large slug of Puligny Montrachet. The first supplicant approached the table.

The mastiffs seated opposite sprung to life. In a gesture reminiscent of John Paul XII, Golden gently raised his left hand to keep them at bay. A jobless film editor came forward and muttered something like, "Hi Andy, long time no see. Hope I'm not disturbing your meal, just wanted to say hello." And though Golden said something pleasant in return, Missy, as the existentialist had addressed Mrs. Golden, fired the solicitor a gunfight-at-the-OK-corral look, which he dodged, and quickly slunk away.

The group in the bar remaining must have agreed between themselves as to the order of presentation, a difficult negotiation, as would be the case between people in parallel pews waiting their turn for confession in a darkened church. The second visitor, an agent known to Golden, introduced a beautiful nymph and her cornucopia of curves. At this interruption, Missy exhaled a long, audible, exasperated sigh. One of the mastiffs rose and strolled over to the bar; words were exchanged.

"This always happens," whispered the existentialist, by way of explanation.

I felt sorry for this crowd; they once must have been something and now thought of themselves as nothing. Their photos would have been at home on milk cartons. None of them seemed prosperous or well, and for all appearances inhabited shanties in the land of ashes presided over by Fitzgerald's Dr. Eckleberger. In fact, I remembered, the Garden of Allah where F. Scott had hunted and pecked his last short stories, was not that far away. I always tried to keep in mind that each human creature is never that far away from Allah's, or whomever's, garden.

The waiter appeared to take orders, and Golden said: "Pollo a la Romana, hold the Romana."

"The usual, eh, Mr. Golden, substitute the mushrooms for the artichokes and just a splash of Marsala?"

"Righto, Jake, and bring a large chopped salad, vinaigrette on the side; everyone can *nosh* on it."

So much for fighting over *hors d'oeuvres*.

I settled on *fettuccine alfredo* with a side of sausage, one of the cheaper dishes on this high-end menu, peasant fare, and the politically correct move. One needs to balance the effrontery of a private plane with a little humility.

When Golden heard this, he asked the waiter to bring the most expensive bottle of *Tignanello* in the restaurant's cellar. A perfect match.

"Collie said you liked old reds," smiled Golden, "old reds, fast women, and slow trains." He glanced knowingly at his wife. "Shall I begin, dear, or would you like to . . . start?"

A rhinestone-like teardrop formed below Missy's left eye. She had been a glove mannequin before marrying up, and well versed in beginnings.

She was unsexy but not unpretty. The patina of expensive clothing and jewelry suggested femininity bartered for the crass and mercantile; an impression not dispelled by well-applied makeup, lip gloss, finely ringed, manicured fingers, and eyelashes that flashed like little scimitars.

"We have only one son," she began.

"I understand you, too, have only one son," said Andrew Golden softly.

"Love him very much," I murmured.

"And our son is . . . well, he is a difficult child . . ."

"Not difficult at all, Mandy. He just has medical problems."

"Andy. You said I could begin. OK?"

"Very well." Andrew Golden rearranged a clump of chopped salad around his plate at the line of scrimmage.

"So. Our son. Sanford. Sandy. We have two children, Brandy and Sandy. Sandy was born prematurely with *spina bifida* and congenital ear infections. He got them again and again, and we didn't know what to do. But the pediatrician recommended, in fact, he ordered, that Sandy do laps in the pool, even before he could swim, with water wings; as therapy for the *spina bifida*. And of course, he couldn't get water in his ears, because that would produce an immediate infection, with high temperatures. He *hated* the pool. So it became a vicious cycle. And we, you know, have very difficult schedules, so we needed to hire a series of nurses, well, first nurses, and then governesses, to monitor these conditions but especially to help him do the pool exercises." She took another gulp from her wine glass.

Andy, Mandy, Brandy, and Sandy. How accessorized, I thought.

"And, you know, you have kids, right? You know how difficult it is to find good help. And Stefan here," and she gestured to the existentialist, "is our *major domo*, don't you see, we would be helpless without him, and he can tell you how difficult it's been to find someone to watch Sandy." Stefan nodded gravely. Had he truly been a stork, he would have stood on one leg and inclined his beak. But he was sitting down, his long legs compressed beneath the table.

"And no matter who we hired, Sandy *hated* them. Absolutely *despised* them, and he refused to eat. It was almost as though he went on hunger strikes. And it may have been because of the pool, because they were required to hold him up, initially as he kicked and stroked, because if he got water in his ear he would get very sick. So he didn't want to go near the pool, but he had to, don't you see, for the *spina bifida?* And he kept *getting* these ear infections. And it was a vicious cycle, isn't it so?"

"To be sure," I nodded in sympathy, "each of my four children tried to die at one time or another, so we are familiar with crises. But please continue."

"I could describe the deficiencies of each one of these governesses, but we would be here all evening. They must have trained at Ringling Brothers. There were *six* who quit or were fired. Sandy tried to bite one of them."

"He didn't *bite* anyone, dear," interrupted Andrew, "the one from Lithuania or Montserrat or wherever shoved a cold, limp, French fry in his mouth . . ."

I decided to throw a block on the reproof forming on

Missy's lips, and asked, "He has an older sister, right, Brandy isn't it? Can't she help care for her little brother?" What an antiquated concept, I thought.

". . . As I was saying. We went through six of these women. No, Brandy is not a maid and is too busy with her acting career. We went through six of these women, and the last one, oh God, the last one . . . and we still don't know if it was an assassination attempt . . ."

"An assassination attempt on a three-year-old child?" I exclaimed in wonder.

"You have no idea how stressful our existence is, Mr. Fitzgerald . . ."

". . . Shane, please, Mrs. Golden . . ."

". . . Then please call me Missy, all the staff does . . ."

"Do we *need* to go into all that, dear, Shane's time is valuable and you are burning it up," said Golden. He poured me a second glass of the *Tignanello* by way of apology for being lumped into their 'staff.' I could already taste the retainer.

The waiter served the entrees. No one touched the food. Missy threw down her fork. "Yes we do. Yes we do. How can we explain the relationship between Nelia and Sandy, otherwise? How can we explain why our child is in . . . is in a . . . *coma?*" and she began to weep uncontrollably. 'The fixer' snaked his arm behind her, drew her close, inviting her to lay her head on his shoulder. Andrew Golden muttered something like, 'goddamn trains, planes, and chicanes' under his breath.

"Look, Shane," said 'the fixer', with undisclosed hostility, "I take it *everything* disclosed at this table remains confidential. You are now a member of the family. Mrs. Golden has agreed to let you call her Missy. You can see the distress this situation has caused." I was already somehow to blame for their torment. I did not dignify his idiotic remark with a reply.

Andrew Golden's doe like eyes morphed into a barn owl glare at 'the fixer', a look that he intended me to notice; we apparently both shared the same opinion of him. So 'the fixer' was *her* guy.

"Would you like me to continue, dear?" he asked, staring at 'the fixer'.

"No, no, no," whined Missy, "you never wanted to go on the trip in the first place; you are prejudiced, and that is not going to help to get Nelia back."

"My mother had a nightmare I would die in an airplane crash," explained Golden sheepishly, "that's why I refuse to fly; maybe that had something to do with the aluminum . . . dart."

Now thoroughly confused, I pulled a blank legal tablet from my briefcase, both to record my impressions of this weird dialogue and to inspire the Goldens to hurry it up. My pilot was not inexpensive, and I hoped to be in bed by midnight; unused, as I was then, to Hollywood hours.

"Perhaps it would be helpful if Shane were given the investigative report," suggested Golden.

Stefan withdrew a sheaf of papers from his valise and handed it to me. This is what it said:

KROLL INVESTIGATIVE SERVICES
WASHINGTON, D.C. BRANCH
500 PENNSYLVANIA AVENUE
WASHINGTON, D.C.

CONFIDENTIAL INVESTIGATIVE REPORT
CONCERNING THE FLIGHT OR ABDUCTION OF
MS. NELIA DOE

PREPARED FOR RATATT, FLISK, & FLIPPIN, LLP,
BEVERLY HILLS, CALIFORNIA
COUNSEL FOR ANDREW GOLDEN PRODUCTIONS

PRELIMINARY

This office was retained by Sherman Flisk, Esq., of the above captioned law firm, to initiate an investigation into the disappearance of a domestic servant employed by Mr. and Mrs. Andrew Golden, of Beverly Hills California, specifically, Nelia Doe (we cannot be sure of, nor have we been able to confirm, her true legal name or identity,) who, until April 1st, 1984, the date of her disappearance, served as governess to Master Sanford Golden, aged 5.

Nelia Doe was hired under unusual circumstances. On June 4th, 1982, there occurred a possible assassination or abduction attempt directed against Master Sanford Golden during hydro-therapy, in the family pool at (redacted address) Beverly Hills, California. At the time, Master Golden was under the supervision and care of Mrs. Priscilla Ramsbottom, former nanny of Charles Windsor (The Prince of Wales.) A splinter of aircraft grade aluminum, perhaps machined for the purpose, either fell from the sky or was launched by slingshot or other means at a water wing supporting Master Golden in the pool. At the time of this event, Master Golden was three years of age, a victim of spina bifida and congenital ear infections, and was not able to swim independent of flotation devices or physical assistance. The shard of aluminum pierced the water wing on his right arm, which deflated, destabilizing him. That caused the water wing on his left arm to detach, causing him to sink to the bottom of the pool. Mrs. Ramsbottom was otherwise distracted and did not see the child go under, but Nelia Doe, who was at that time employed by 'A Very Nice Pool Company' of Westwood, California, and was preparing to clean the pool, saw the event and dove into the pool, rescued him, and administered some sort of primitive CPR. Mr. Golden came upon the scene soon thereafter, investigated what had taken place, terminated Mrs. Ramsbottom, and that day hired Nelia Doe at a salary three times her hourly take-home pay at 'A Very Nice Pool Company'. Before doing so, he obtained the permission of the pool company, explaining that Master Golden had become immediately emotionally attached to Nelia Doe, and could not bear to be out of her sight. Nelia gave the Goldens a copy of the same false Social Security Card that she had presented to the pool company.

The source of the aluminum splinter has never been determined. There are, at all times, at least four security guards on duty at the Golden home in Beverly Hills, and on that day both Stefan Zweig, who manages domestic affairs for Mr. and Mrs. Golden, and Mrs. Golden's secretary were present in the home. The swimming pool is protected by dense foliage, which did not appear to have been disturbed. Moreover, neither Mrs. Ramsbottom nor Nelia Doe saw anyone lurking in the foliage or any object fly overhead. The Golden mansion is not in the glide path of either LAX or Burbank Airport. The Beverly Hills Police Department performed a routine investigation, and, thereafter, the Kroll office in Beverly Hills performed a full and thorough investigation, as a result of Mrs. Golden's dissatisfaction with the conclusions reached by the Beverly Hills Police. The progress of that investigation is contained in report ABG765554 which is on file with counsel Flisk. After Ms. Doe's hire as governess, Master Golden began to thrive. Mrs. Golden reports that his appetite improved, he ceased resistance to the pool exercises, since Nelia Doe physically supported him throughout, and his disposition markedly improved. The congenital ear infections ceased. In 1983, Sandy accompanied the family to their beach house in Malibu, and played in the surf under the supervision of Nelia Doe.

In the winter of 1983, Mrs. Golden began planning a family trip to Washington, D.C., based on an invitation by the President and his wife to lunch at the White House. Mr. Golden does not fly, so ground transportation was secured between Los Angeles and Washington, D.C. As the trip evolved Mrs. Golden added a sea voyage to Great Britain, and thereafter, a limousine-ferryboat leg to France, where Mrs. Golden wished to bring the children to see Monet's garden in Giverny, Versailles, and Parisian museums, particularly, the Louvre and the Museé D'Orsai, where one of the Goldens' Monets was at that time on loan. Elizabeth Windsor (The Queen of England) extended an invitation to visit Balmoral Castle in Scotland, as she is a great fan of the *Nepotism* series, in which Lady Carter Bonham Rhees, daughter of one of the ladies-in-waiting to the Queen, appears. Travel between Southampton, where the family would initially disembark in Great Britain, and Balmoral Castle in Scotland where the Queen would be in residence, would be by private train.

The security arrangements for this trip, which was to take, all told, two months, inclusive of ground and sea travel, were complex. This office was retained to provide security en route across the country, in Washington, D.C., in London, and in Paris. The Queen's staff would provide security at Balmoral.

Mrs. Golden arranged for three sleeping cars, one for her and Mr. Golden, a second for the children and their governesses, and a third for staff, including security, a fully equipped kitchen car, a dining car, an observation car, a car equipped with video games and television sets for the children, and a production office car so that Mr. Golden could continue his work while en route to New York. These cars would be drawn by two locomotives, tenders, and the like. The train consisted of twenty-three locomotives, tenders, cars, and cabooses all told. Complex logistics governed the switching of tracks between Los Angeles and Washington D.C.

Upon arrival in Washington, D.C., the family would stay at the British Embassy by invitation by the Queen; thereafter, at the Pierre in New York, prior to the family's embarkation on the QEII. After some difficult negotiation, Mrs. Golden was able to book the Sun Deck of the QEII for both the New York – South Hampton eastbound and westbound legs of the sea voyage. Other passengers were to be excluded from this deck, which included twelve luxury suites, a cinema in which Mr. Golden could view rushes (which would be dropped by Falcon Jet with signal buoys for retrieval by the ship's crew for each of the six days of the voyage), a private grill and dining room, and an exercise pavilion. The train would leave Los Angeles during the first week of June, in order to arrive in Washington in time for the Reagan luncheon, and, thereafter, to be on hand for the sailing of the QEII on June 15th, 1984.

During the last week in February of 1984, Stefan Zweig, Chief of Staff for the Golden Family, asked the various domestic servants, and, specifically, the two governesses of the children, for their passports, so that he could check their validity and obtain the requisite visas for Great Britain and France, for those servants who were not United States Citizens. Nelia Doe, with whom Mr. Zweig enjoyed a close relationship, seemed perplexed and anguished at this request, but said she would comply. By the second week of March, when she had not produced the requested passport, Mr. Zweig approached Ms. Doe again, and, at this point, she broke down in tears and indicated she had no passport, could get no passport, and could not leave the United States. This news was conveyed to Mrs. Golden, who then indicated to Nelia that a substitute nanny would be found for Master Golden for this trip, and Nelia would have to remain in Beverly Hills for its two-month duration. Once informed that Nelia would not be coming on the trip, the child grew anxious, stopped eating, could not sleep, and began to experience a recrudescence of his symptoms. He announced he did not want to go on the trip without Ms. Doe. When Mr. Golden heard this news, he indicated that he would not go on the trip without his son, and that the 'girls' could go on the trip without him, Mrs. Golden responded that this would be 'unacceptable'; she had already spent USD $1.3 million (One million three hundred thousand United States Dollars), on non-refundable deposits for both the train and the QEII, and she would not lose this money. Moreover, the Reagans and the Queen were expecting to see Mr. Golden. Mrs. Golden asserted that Mr. Golden had never wished to go on the trip in the first place; acrimony and, apparently, a great deal of disruption, occurred in the household at this time, witnessed by Ms. Doe, and, on or about April 1st, 1984, she disappeared. It should be noted that the usual background investigation check was not performed by this office prior to Ms. Doe's hire, so the Goldens had no idea of her status. It should also be noted that she is a woman of about 6'2" in height with very dark skin, well-muscled, with very short hair. She is not unattractive. Her disappearance produced several untoward consequences: Master Golden, upon realizing that Ms. Doe was gone, and might not return, fell into a comatose state from which he has not emerged. He is fed intravenously under the care of round-the-clock nurses and a pediatrician, who have set up a hospital room in the Golden mansion. Mr. Golden has blamed this circumstance on the extravagance of Mrs. Golden's intended trip, and her shouting at Ms. Nelia Doe when the passport was not forthcoming; Mrs. Golden rejoined that it should not have been that difficult to obtain a passport for the governess, and wished to terminate Mr. Zweig. Mr. Golden refused to terminate Mr. Zweig. This office has discovered the following circumstances, which may (or may not) have prompted Ms. Doe to flee:

1. We have learned, from an interview of personnel at 'A Very Nice Pool Company' (who were most cooperative), and an examination of paperwork and other personal effects left in Ms. Doe's room when she fled, particularly, from a meticulous journal that she left behind, that in January of 1981 Ms. Doe hired a self-styled immigration specialist, Hyman Gutterman, Esq., of Gardena, California, to process paperwork so that she could become a legal immigrant. The Social Security Number she had given 'A Very Nice Pool Company' proves to be that of one Sonya Valles, a Mexican National with whom we have been unable to make contact. It is clear that Ms. Doe did not have and does not have a valid Social Security Number. Nor, for that matter, does Ms. Doe have a valid California Driver License or Identification Card. In short, it would appear that she was and is an illegal immigrant.

2. Receipts found in Ms. Doe's personal effects disclose that she paid Gutterman a retainer of USD $1,000.00 (one thousand dollars) to process an application for legal residence. Other than that, it appears her monthly salary was remitted to family members in Belize. Those family members were contacted by this office but disclaim any knowledge of her whereabouts. As will be seen, infra, Gutterman arranged a bogus marriage for her with a heroin addict named Jeffrey Scales. Confidential sources reveal that Jeffrey Scales has three State misdemeanor convictions and one State felony conviction for possession of a controlled substance, to wit, heroin. Scales and Ms. Doe obtained a marriage license from the Clerk of the County of Los Angeles Santa Monica Office

on March 2nd, 1981. In the application for marriage license Scales gives his address as 1043 W. 105th Street, Los Angeles, California (which is the south central district of Los Angeles known as Watts), and Ms. Doe listed the same address. Neither party can be traced to that address. Ms. Doe apparently never revealed her true address (unknown to this office) to either the attorney Gutterman or to the Immigration and Naturalization Service, nor, of the name and address of her then employer, 'A Very Nice Pool Company'. Records searched in four different counties of the State of California (Los Angeles, San Joaquin, San Bernardino, and Kern) show that Scales has been married six times, and that his last known marriage, to one Carmela Contreras, of Venice Beach, California, was not terminated at the time he obtained the most recent marriage license. Ms. Doe and Scales were married in Las Vegas, Nevada on March 3rd, 1981.

3. INS FOIA (Freedom of Information Act) and the Affidavit of Carl Colson, Special Agent of the Federal Bureau of Investigation, in Support of Search Warrant, a non-public document obtained by this office, indicate that on March 9th, 1981, Gutterman filed, on behalf of Ms. Doe, a form 1-130 (Petition to Classify Alien Relative) and I-485 (Petition for Adjustment of Status) with the Immigration and Naturalization Service Office in Los Angeles California. Thereafter, on March 23rd, 1981, a notice was sent to 'Mr. and Mrs. Jeffrey Scales' at the Watts address for an interview on Thursday, May 17th, 1981 at INS headquarters in Los Angeles. Gutterman was sent a copy of this notice at his Gardena office.

4. On the morning of May 17th, Gutterman showed up for the interview, but his clients did not. Gutterman was confronted with the fact that Scales had been married six times previous, all to foreign nationals, that Gutterman had processed immigration filings for two of his prior alien wives, and, in fact, handled Scales' divorces after the wives had received immigration papers. The case was referred to the FBI, which obtained a search warrant for Gutterman's office, where receipts for cash payments made to Scales were seized, but no receipts or other records of monies received from Nelia Doe aka Consuelo Contreras. Warrants for the arrest of

Gutterman, Scales and Nelia Doe were issued by the Federal District Court in and for the Southern District of California in late 1983. Gutterman was apprehended and bail set at USD $500,000.00 (five hundred thousand US dollars). He has not met bail and is in custody awaiting trial, on in excess of forty counts of mail fraud, money laundering, and various violations of criminal law sections of the Immigration and Naturalization statutes. Nelia Doe and Scales are charged as co-conspirators engaging in a fraudulent marriage to obtain Immigration Benefits, a felony, and, listed as material witnesses against Gutterman.

5. It is not known, whether or not, Ms. Doe was made aware of the charges against her; however, her papers do not show she received notice of the hearing at INS and it is presumed she might have become suspicious, at some point, that things had not gone well in her immigration case. It is possible that Gutterman never informed her of the interview. It is also more likely than not that Stefan Zweig, if not Mr. and Mrs. Golden, was at all times aware of Ms. Doe's irregular status, because she was paid only in cash, and no deductions (Federal or State of California) were calculated or made. This is a particularly sensitive issue in view of the pending investigation against Mrs. Ronald Reagan's personal maid, Anita Sanabria Castelo, for smuggling munitions to Paraguay. Though there is no particular evidence that Ms. Doe and Ms. Castelo know or knew each other (though indeed they were together at the Goldens' beach house during one Presidential visit there), Mr. Golden does not wish any adverse publicity to befall either the President or the Golden family due to their hiring of aliens. In response to Counsel Flisk's question as to whether Ms. Doe might benefit from the Simpson-Mazzoli Amnesty Legislation pending before the Congress, we would defer that question to specialized Immigration and Naturalization Counsel.

6. Ms. Doe's wallet and handbag are no longer present in her room; Mr. Zweig has opined that employment motivated her immigration to the United States, because she is the sole support of a young daughter in Belize, the country of her origin. It is not known whether she or her daughter are nationals of Belize, or of Mexico, though Mr. Golden has

indicated she has a 'Harry Belafonte' accent, which would indicate she might be of Creole origin. Mr. Zweig has seen a photograph of the young daughter, kept in Ms. Doe's wallet, which is no longer available. The family has no photograph which shows Nelia Doe's full face but there are a number of security camera films which depict her performing her chores as a nanny.

7. On or about May 1st, Nelia Doe placed a call from, apparently, somewhere in Northern Mexico to Zweig's private number at the mansion. No one was available to take the call, however, a phone recording of the message was made. It has been transcribed as follows:

Nelia Doe: "Ummmmmm . . . Hi, Stefan, I am Nelia here. Is Sandy OK? I had to run or they will deport me anyway. I am really calling about Sandy. I am sure Mr. and Missy will fire me by now, but I don't have a passport, couldn't get one from nowhere. Tried to contact the lawyer, he is *un cabron*; apparently, they have him in the jail. Good. But they might put me in with him or send me back to Belize. Hi. Tell Sandy love him. Don't know what I can do. Bye."

Then there is a recording of a whining or barking of a small dog. We discovered that pay phone calls from the city of Chihuahua, in the state of Chihuahua, Northern Mexico, are ended by a recording of the yapping of a Chihuahua dog of similar origin. So we think that Nelia Doe is somewhere in Chihuahua, Chihuahua, Mexico, in hiding.

(Report continues, p 6.)

I looked up from the paper at this point; having read quite enough. Stefan Zweig politely reached for it and inserted it between the soft flaps of a fine, black leather Italian case from which it had come. Apparently, I'd not yet been 'approved.'

"The doctors say unless she can come back and Sandy can hear her voice he might die," blubbered Missy. "Shane, Shane, if it were *your* son how would you feel? You should see him, his face so white, his lips are blue . . ."

"And if you can do nothing, Shane," said Andrew Golden kindly, "just say so. Our own lawyers have thrown up their hands. We pay these bastards millions of dollars a year to handle various matters and . . ."

"They were the ones who represented us when the Federal Government raided the studio and seized film cans of the *Milton Mephistopheles* pilot, when . . ." blurted Missy.

'The fixer' treated me to the kind of look the mako must have given Santiago's fish: If you don't take the case, we don't get our cut; we will go elsewhere, of course, but if you take the case and fail – well, no soup for you.

"Mandy, let's stay on track here," said Golden, and to me, "What are your thoughts?"

"You folks certainly *do* lead complex lives. Well, let's think it out for a moment. Requires some reflection." I had not touched the *alfredo* with its sausage side. The anguish at the table killed everyone's appetite.

"And I take it you not only want her back in one piece, *presto chango,* but you want her to accompany Sandy on this trip, and afterwards, be admitted *back* into the United States?"

"Optimally," responded Andrew Golden, "but the trip is beside the point. What the hell," and he glanced at Missy, "are forfeitable trip deposits compared to the health of a child?"

"But it would be *ideal,*" she rejoined, "If you could do that. Can you *do* that? There would be a substantial bonus involved if you could *do* that."

"I don't know."

"I mean," she argued, glancing at 'the fixer', "the trip would be *good* for Sandy, the culture, and all that."

"The solution to this is a little like a recipe for *Crème*

brûlée; no, it is more like a recipe for a soufflé," I murmured. Comparing the problem to expensive French desserts was good salesmanship.

"How so?" asked Andrew Golden.

"Well, if you blow any one step, the whole production falls. You've been there, right, Mr. Golden?"

"Andy."

"Andy. Right. The Kroll folks are the best, are they not? Imagine discovering that the whining dog or whatever is a promotion for Mexitel?"

"And we understand you are fluent in Spanish, and have a Hispanic paralegal on staff."

I nodded. I did have one of those. But how did *they* know this?

"But, among other things, there's a slight conflict of interest, isn't there? After all, if we are successful in persuading the governess to come back, assuming we could get her across the border, young Sandy may awake from his torpor but Ms. Doe will be arrested. And, if, after hundreds of thousands of dollars in legal fees and multiple procedures, she happens to be convicted, and has to spend hard time, then what have we accomplished for the young man?"

"He will be much older then," said Mandy, "and not so dependent. We were foolish to allow him to become so attached in the first place." She must have forgotten his current condition.

"Conflicts of interest?" mused Golden, "Where is the conflict of interest in saving the life of a child? Oh, I see . . . you mean, who is your real client?"

"Exactly. Who *is* my real client?"

"Well, *I* am the client, young man: if you do your work

correctly, everyone benefits. If you don't, the damage is catastrophic, both to my son, and to Nelia."

"No pressure at all, eh?"

I could give Andrew and Mandy Golden neither the comfort of an answer, nor the panacea of false hope. Andy insisted that, before returning to Santa Monica airport, we pay a brief visit to the mansion to look in on the comatose boy. His reputation as an alchemist of emotional engagement was well earned. We had a chance encounter with Brandy Golden, a sullen eleven year old glued to a television set watching a rerun of Marilyn Monroe in *The Misfits*. If she weren't careful, she would grow up to look exactly like Erica Jong. Might even have to sell sex tapes.

Though her father introduced me quickly as 'the man who might be able to help save Sandy,' the girl barely acknowledged my presence.

The little boy, his face bluish-white like a marble cherub, lay propped on a hospital bed in a well-lighted room, connected to monitoring devices. The room gave off 'white' sound punctuated by bleeps. Two uniformed nurses sat on either side of the headboard reading page turners; there was nothing else for them to do. And perhaps there would be nothing anyone could do.

Golden and I returned to the airport alone. He drew on his pipe, stared into the darkness and said, "You know, don't you, that this girl is blacker than Collie; she won't be easy to find in Mexico. But you can be sure she's a damn side taller than any Mexican you'll encounter there!" He gave me a strong hug resembling thanks. "You strike me as the kind of guy that doesn't make snap decisions, promise things you can't deliver. And you have kids of your own. Think about it and let us know."

His chauffeur handed up to the pilot a to-go bag with the now glutinous *fettuccine alfredo* and a bottle of wine.

"There's two orders in the bag, in case you had nothing while waiting," Golden said to the pilot.

My Cessna ascended into the silver, black, chartreuse-tinted night and was soon sandwiched in velvet nothingness between the kaleidoscopic lightscape of Los Angeles after dark, and a bright tiara of cut diamond stars.

I liked Golden, and helping the little boy would be deeply satisfying. As to Missy – well, as to Missy, I glanced out the window to make sure her broom was not trailing the aircraft.

I was glad to escape Southern California, wondering how much simpler life would be selling mangoes for a living, on a street corner in San Jose, Costa Rica. I donned a pair of earphones, turning up the volume of Kiri Te Kanawa singing *Un Bel Di* until she drowned the hum of the plane's Lycoming engines, and I fell asleep.

CHAPTER V

CAYA ESMERALDA II

The evening before my rendezvous with Mr. Inevitable, I took a long shower in the staff wash-up room, scrubbing my skin with a stone and coconut oil until it glowed. I towel dried my hair for maximum curl. I applied just a touch of silver eyeliner and lip gloss from a make-up kit given to me by a female guest, and lay in my hammock waiting for my roommates to cease their chatter and begin their snorting and snoring. I found myself vibrating.

At last, I slipped through the night in a black cotton nightgown trying to walk stealthily and rhythmically as an Egyptian, *Nine Stories* in one hand, the key and a net bag filled with this and that in the other. I could tell by the back lit clouds and the closed hibiscus blossoms it must be 2:00 a.m. I did not timidly knock at the door of his suite like a beggar. I used the key, which turned smoothly in the lock, and entered the suite.

He reclined on a divan in white cotton shorts and white polo shirt open at the neck, sweat bands on his wrists and head as though he had just walked off a tennis court. But we didn't have one on Caya Esmeralda. In the total darkness of the room he glowed phosphorescently, like breaking waves. Perhaps his appearance was intended as a greeting. Beside him, twinkling in the light from the open door, Bilisters sweated in an iced hamper. He did not rise, as if such a move would break his control. What *did* he intend? A master-servant relationship? My blood began to rise.

"Well hello there, Desireé," he said pleasantly, without a hint of surprise, "what is your real name, since everyone on this fantasy island seems to have adopted fake ones?"

"I'm not supposed to tell you, and we do not get to know

yours," I replied, crisply. "We can be fired for asking. While diving, when a shark approaches, it doesn't usually announce, 'I am a shark.' What troubles you about the name Desireé?"

"So you are *afraid* of sharks . . ."

". . . Not at *all.*"

". . . This is not a *carcel,* you know, what do you propose to call *me*?"

I sat down across from him on a hassock, without crossing my legs, and folded my hands in my lap. I remember the hem of my black nightgown tickling my bare feet and thinking, maybe I should have painted my toes. But I knew he would not forget the shape of my legs from my walk away at the pool the other day.

"I will just think of you as 'Mr. Inevitable'."

He told me later he had watched, carefully, my body language for three days, which inspired this line from the mouth of one of his future literary characters: 'She reminded him of an unbroken colt that had pitched off many a rider. She might buck off one more. But his intuition told him that, handled carefully, she could be ridden.'

"So what did you think of the stories?"

"Well, I read them all once. And then, I read them again. I do not understand everything. Why does the banana fish bloke think it a good idea to shoot himself?"

"Well, it ends the story, doesn't it? If you study Salinger's characters, you can tell he is hung up somewhere between his Jewishness and Irishness, compounded by the trauma of his D–Day landing. There always must be a kind of violent ending. That is why he eats organic peas and underdone lamb patties and lives like a hermit, because he believes he will get out of here alive, though his characters are never so lucky."

"There is no creature under heaven such as a banana fish, now, is there?"

"I'm glad you got that part of it. No, but banana fish are similes – or metaphors – in more simple words, examples of hypocrisy and greed. Imagine old Florida widows with blue veined legs and orange hair swarming around the blintz station during Sunday brunch at the Doral, gorging themselves."

I did not comprehend these comparisons and said so.

"Like old ladies in a market fighting over the ripest mangoes."

I drew closer to him, removed a Churchill cigar from my net bag, carefully peeled away the cellophane wrapper, and began to prepare it, as taught by my manager. A sensual striptease using the cigar as a symbol. I didn't know whether he smoked them, and didn't care. He watched my hazel eyes studying the cigar. I attempted to clip its end with sterling silver Dunhill device, and failing in that, just bit it off and spat into the darkness. He smiled at me as if to ask if other guests been serviced in this manner.

"You don't need to do that," he said, dismissively. "You must have many boyfriends."

Did he mean this as an insult, or a question? He looked far too cool, comfortable, and self-assured.

"And you must have as many wives."

That didn't rattle him.

"Do I *look* Muslim? One wife, four children."

"Most men are afraid of me, that's why."

"That's why *what*?"

"You might say," trying to read his mind, "I am a fast car that has never been driven."

"Ah, a version of a virgin."

"Something like."

"Well, I have never taken a *fast* car, as you put it, for its first test drive. So now I must be at least as scared as you are."

"You could pretend to be a *little* scared; I bit a chunk from a bloke's arm once. I am not used to men who are unafraid. And why did you choose this particular book from your . . . stack . . . for me?"

"I think they are interesting stories. They are what we call 'cautionary tales', written by an old guy who enjoys preying on young women, about old guys preying on young women. So I'm doing you a favor, really."

"I think you gave it to me to try to seduce me. It is a house full of Trojans."

He doubled over in laughter, glancing at the vanity at bedside.

"It's worked so far, hasn't it? I'm 35, you're, what, 18? You're in my room, after all."

I had to smile. If this was what the American magazines scavenged by maids from trashcans described as 'foreplay,' it was a kind of delicious fun, like slicing a mango and turning it inside out so it turns into cubes

"So, when you scribble and scrabble while everyone else is out diving or walking on the beach, what are you aiming for?"

"Spying on me, eh? All lawyers are frustrated novelists."

"And what are you writing about?"

"Just poems, actually. And one short story."

"Can I see them?"

"No, you'll just dismiss them as instruments of seduction."

I lowered my head and tried to give him what I now know is called an 'opaque' look.

"Will you ever write a story about me?"

"That will depend upon what kind of life you live, whether you have adventures which are worth recording. Love and squalor, and all that."

He must have wanted to be sure I had read the story about Esmé and her soldier.

"Yes, what *does* the girl mean by 'love and squalor?'"

"She is a young girl, but an old spirit; her little brother is the tennis net over which she and the protagonist (I should say, 'the old guy') volley their little seductions. The author's meaning is clear: love inevitably leads to squalor; you will learn that."

"The writer must be a miserable old bugger, to think that way."

"You have to make yourself crazy to write well, or let other people, or life, torture you to madness; you have to drive right to the edge of the abyss with the intention of going over without actually doing so, like James Dean in *Rebel Without a Cause*, unlike a writer named Sylvia Plath, who eventually souffléed her brains in an oven. To court seduction is to beckon danger; the moth *inevitably* becomes crisped by the flame."

Well, fair play to him. That sounded truthful. I was prepared to be crisped. But I pretended to consider his warning for a few seconds while ruffling the pages of the book and looking out the window into the dark leaves glittering in the moonlight.

"When will I learn about love and squalor?"

The strap of my black nightgown had slipped two inches below my left shoulder blade. I made no attempt to shrug it back into position. I imagined how it looked there, what it might say about that little pinch of flesh between my bicep and breast.

"Well, you have made one hell of a beginning, reading the books . . . and coming here tonight."

"Give me a *chinchi* Bilister, then," I smiled.

"Maybe you will need a brandy."

"I don't drink that hard stuff – touch my skin. It is like velvet."

And like an idiot, I offered up the skin of my forearm.

"I have a suggestion," he opened a leather case on the glass coffee table, "do you play chess?"

"I have done," I admitted.

"Well, let's play for stakes. Strip chess."

"*Cho*! No way. Wicked man."

"It's not what you think."

"No," I said, standing up, intending to bolt.

"The rules are, for every piece *I* win, you drink a Bilister and one swig of brandy. For every piece *you* win, I will remove one article of clothing. From me, that is."

He must have guessed I had but one article to shed.

"And what does the loser have to do?"

"You are not intending on losing, are you?"

"No. But if I do, then what?"

"Then . . . nothing."

"There is never nothing, there is always something."

"Nothing will happen that you don't want to happen."

I sat down again, folded my hands in my lap. Then, as a sort of warning to him, or perhaps to myself, I picked up the book and read, from its last page:

'He was little more than halfway down the staircase when he heard an all piercing sustained scream – clearly coming from a small, female child. It was highly acoustical, as though it were reverberating within four tiled walls.'

He began setting up the pieces on the board as though nothing unusual had been said.

"How does the story really end, is what I want to know."

He considered this question for a moment, apparently trying to remember if Teddy killed Booper by pushing her into the empty swimming pool on the cruise ship, if Booper killed Teddy by pushing him into the pool, or if Teddy committed suicide. He either couldn't remember, didn't know, or didn't want *me* to know that *he* didn't know, so he said: "It is irrelevant, isn't it? Salinger is just doing a Zen reincarnation trip on the reader. If we know everything, if our cells are preprogrammed with all knowledge, and if we transubstantiate into different forms, then, who the hell cares who dies?"

"I don't understand *any* of that. But I *care* about the characters. I want to know."

"Well, I *think* Teddy commits suicide, and that's why the little sister screams. Too much knowledge is a dangerous thing, particularly, too much self-knowledge."

"Do you have a backgammon set?"

"Why?"

"It's a faster game."

"You in a big rush?"

"Can you hear the hooyu yellin' outside? That means it's 3:00 a.m. We have only a few hours of darkness left."

Hooyu racketing in the bushes; waiting to fly at you like ghosts if you walked the strand too late, whizzing by like the United States fighter jets blasting over Belize, as though they own it.

"How did you learn to play backgammon?"

"By watchin' people at the bar. And the dice are black and white. They will let us know if you are more black than white, or I am more white than black."

"Which is something that neither of us really needs to know."

"That's *one* of the things you really want to know, isn't it? It's maybe the only thing you will take away from this."

He told me later I reminded him then of how he didn't want his daughters to grow up to be: exotic, a little wild, somewhat homegrown. He wanted his daughters to grow up refined, logical, restrained, country clubbish, razor minded, questioning authority. He wanted them to become Sturdy Golden Bears at Berkeley without a hint of sexual liberation. But he didn't feel compelled to act as an example when this far from home; enjoyed smashing up suburban conventions as much as I enjoyed burning catechisms.

So he located his traveling backgammon set ('All lawyers have them', he said) and we tossed the dice to see who would roll first. Though the dice favored him, it was the beginning of the end. First his left wristband came off, then the right, then the sweatband, then his polo shirt, then his shoes and socks, and finally, his shorts. I did not place these winnings in a neat pile by my side, but flung them in various corners of the room, where it would be difficult for him to retrieve them. I drank three beers in rapid succession with brandy chasers to minimize the pain between my legs I hoped would come. I didn't linger over them; they reminded me of medicine. I was close to skunking him, what they call 'gammoning' him, when I decided to preserve his ego like they caution girls in magazines. So I stood up and stretched my arms toward the ceiling, feeling the air from the white fan blades ripple the long ringlets of my hair. I stretched backward, knotting my bow.

"There must also be a prize for the loser." I said. "But first, I have to pee."

I walked into the WC and, without closing the door, hiked up my black nightgown, *stood* on the loo like we were taught in the mission school, and peed.

He had discipline. Though unmasked, his equipment did not spring to attention. I didn't need to look for stretch marks or scars. Only women got those; his poor wife must look like a gunny sack.

He used my absence to move from the divan to the large, low-slung bed behind louvered doors. He lay down and began to sing:

> *'Your eyelashes tickle my nose*
> *you close your cover before striiiiking*
> *you're eyes are like limpid oysters*
> *loving you has made me bananas.'*

I walked over to the bed, stood there, laughed at his weird song, shrugged my shoulders and the shift curtained down.

". . . *'Foaming like a wave on the ground around her knees'* . . ." he murmured.

"I read where humans in the Middle East ban those body parts which are best."

"It is always a difficult decision for them."

He picked up another legal pad lying on the bed and recited: "antibiotics, beef jerky, the Big Doughnut, circumstantial evidence, cherries, cunnilingus, deceptions, epigrams (of two types: venal come-ons and prohibitions in the Baltimore Catechism), fellatio, flashbulbs, fondling, gonorrhea (and all STDS), hell, judgment day, kimchee, lovers (entwined), morels, Nubians, 'O, The Story Of', pink tongued terriers, prophylactics (raincoats), raincoats (prophylactics), slavery, tender uncooked Kobe beef, underwear (or her lack thereof), virgins, wife in tears, yikes, zygotes." What a weird mind he had.

What I felt, thought about, didn't write down, and now have a hard time remembering: orchids, bends, bulges, catfish, barbells, curiosity, gumption, diving deeply, Easter, fear, fired, goose pimples, Hook, the Holy Ghost, lack of oxygen, La Valentina, knifes, lust, bulls mounting heifers, priests, queasy, shame, sharks . . . and wetness.

"You have the body of a Nilotic priestess, the long muscles of a swimmer, a very narrow waist, a David ass, and . . . those lovely orbs," and he reached up to touch my breasts, "nuzzle each other like bluebells. A geometrician would have a field day with the curves and parabolas of your body." He paused. "We could have the usual discussion about sexually transmitted diseases and what we are going to do about those."

'Nilotic, David ass, orbs?' And the multi-syllabic words he loved to throw around: 'circumstantial, cunnilingus, fellatio, geometrician, gonorrhea, parabolas, prophylactics, prohibitions.' I arranged them in my mind to record in my journal later if I got out of there alive.

"Shut your mouth," I told him. "I'm not one of your lily-girl *putas*. If you're clean, I have no fear. I just want to know everything you know."

I sat beside him on the bed, ran my fingers through his golden hair.

"I have been longing to know," I said, "whether it feels like dry corn stalk or like sea grass."

He drew from the drawer of the commode beside the bed a condom wrapped like a Roman coin with a soldier on it, branded 'Trojan', and held it up. Ah. Then I got the joke about the stupid wooden horse. I suddenly worried if he had been with one of my *provinciana* roommates.

I gave him a look of disgust. "I have never eaten the skin before the banana, have you?"

I knew there were two sides to this coin. I could sense him thinking about his wife.

"For an inexperienced young lady, you do rap right along."

"I've read too many magazines," I smiled. "But I have no diseases."

He put the condom back in the drawer.

"Come here," he said, and drew me to him, "don't worry, I won't pull out a pack of cigarettes afterwards."

We lay facing each other.

"So what is it all that you want to learn?" he asked kindly, stroking my cheek.

I didn't know what to tell him. Actions speak louder than words.

This proved to be the most tender of all my nights.

CHAPTER VI

DRAKES BEACH, POINT REYES, CALIFORNIA

It can be useful, when overcome with extra-human stress (the scourge of all professionals' lives), or, when seeking answers to apparently insoluble dilemmas, to go for long runs on deserted beaches. I remember (vaguely) an essay by Einstein about how the great man, when unable to solve the seeming incongruities of the time/space warp, retreated to his study and played the violin. Relativity then revealed itself to his subconscious.

My running course is a two-mile crescent of sand beneath the bluffs Sir Francis Drake christened 'New Albion', now Drake's Bay, not in sight of The Farallons, home-court of the great white shark. If one draws a line perpendicular from the white-crested bluffs, it will bear almost due East. Off-putting, for one who grew up on Southern California shores facing west. So don't make the same mistake as Drake and think you are in San Francisco Bay; this body of water is part of the feeding ground of those great whites, known to chase seals into its placid waters. From which, if you are a seal, there is no escape.

I crossed the Richmond San Rafael Bridge, then drove through a redwood forest along a twisting road molded to the curves of a small stream, as far as Point Reyes National Seashore and Drake's Bay, its farthest extremity. I shed my dark blue sweat suit for running shorts and shoes, and took off along the strand. The irony of running between cougars, which still roamed the bluffs, and the greatest collection of marine predators on the planet did not escape me. The occasional decapitated seal carcass proved the 'Do Not Swim, Dangerous Riptides and Sharks' sign was not just another bureaucratic terror trinket. During this run I came upon some *echinarachniae parmae*, sand dollars, or, more accurately, sand dimes. I pocketed one and, exhausted, sat down facing the sea and placed it on the sand between my legs. I picked up a small driftwood stick.

I sweated out untold tales in my subconscious, their characters conceived but yet unborn. I began with an organizational chart of the characters. It was so much easier to depict them in sand, as the recordations of my feeble markings would be washed away by the power of the sea. There would be no emails to anyone concerning this matter. There would indeed be no fee agreement, though the rules of the State Bar called for one. Golden said he didn't need one, didn't want one. What if I failed at this current assignment? A question that every lawyer, every film producer, every entrepreneur, every politician, always asks. I could imagine the venomous 'fixer' lurking in a tray of figs to bite me on the nipple. I could imagine Collie infecting me with a bureaucratic lymphoma that could lead to disbarment. What if the little kid died before the mysterious Nelia Doe could be retrieved? Worse, what if I never *found* her. And *before* I found her, I had to put her through an annulment proceeding. How did one do *that?* But Golden's $100K retainer was safe and sweltering in my trust account, and it covered a multitude of sins. Hungry mouths clamored to devour it.

The sand dollar served as a compass rose, a lodestar, from which I drew lines in the sand radiating from the markings on its carapace. Had I connected their ends I could have formed a circle, but I did not do that; I craved unbroken linear logic. I wondered if Andrew Golden saw life as a pattern of grays, or whether *he* made decisions based on perceptions of the greater moral good, not dictated by stale precepts, hollow logic, moldering statutes. I ended one straight line with a squiggle. I hoped I was the kind of lawyer who would not only bend the law to suit the needs of a client, but shatter it like a chicken bone if strict adherence to dusty tomes guaranteed an immoral outcome.

My ego could not stand being perceived as a loser. Such perceptions were anathema to me, because the good ol' biological father had tried to cut my leg off with a kitchen knife, in infancy – a life history which can tend to make one feel unworthy and insecure.

And I would not put either the client or myself through the time, expense, attrition, and sheer bullshit necessary to invalidate a cumbersome statute. Neither was I the kind of lawyer who would bankrupt a client by writing four or five hundred page briefs to challenge a statute in a lower court, lose, appeal that loss, lose, and take the matter to the State or Federal Supreme Court. It was too much goddamned work and no fun. I would perform the task swiftly and surgically, or not at all. I presumed Andrew Golden had selected me to try to save the life of his son because he knew what was necessary to get the job done *would* be done, with maximum courage and a little flare. Cost or personal risk be damned.

All righty, then.

I scraped at the sand with the stick. And began to scribble.

'The first thing I must do', I concluded, 'is to *cut* or *loosen* the federal noose the shyster placed around Nelia's neck.' How to accomplish this? The marriage was indeed a fraud, and, in California, a fraudulent marriage may be annulled. If the marriage is annulled, then it never existed, and if it never existed, then intent to evade immigration laws by engaging in a fraudulent marriage can never be proved – even if Nelia harbored such a specific intent; which would be unusual in a domestic servant. I vaguely remembered that a petition for an annulment could be filed in any county of California, as opposed to one for dissolution, which must be filed in the county where the parties to the marriage resided. But how to file an annulment without a plaintiff who could appear, live, on the stand? In those days, law was practiced using live people, as opposed to cyborgs. Well, Andrew Golden had plenty of actresses in his stable. And I knew a friendly female judge in Contra Costa County, one of California's first lesbian judges, a judge who danced to the beat of different drums. The annulment was the *first* thing to be done.

The second thing that must be done is to present a Federal Prosecutor with a decree of annulment, which would force him to dismiss the indictment against Nelia.

Third, she must be found in Mexico and persuaded that the threat of imprisonment in the United States had been eliminated.

Fourth, we must get her a passport. She had obviously been unable to do this on her own.

Fifth, with the passport in hand, pressure need be applied on some United States consul to issue her *some* sort of visa, a visa sufficient to get her *back* into the United States. For this part of the scheme, a 'bag of tricks' would be needed, because her various illegalities included working in the United States, no doubt under a false social security number, and the U.S. Consulate would only issue her a tourist visa *if she did not intend to work. A specific purpose* for such a visit must be demonstrated, such as the need for a medical treatment not available in Mexico, or required attendance at a special event. This would present a significant problem because the Reagan administration ran a pretty straight immigration show, particularly when it came to insulating the President. No special influence *whatsoever* could be used.

Sixth, tourist visas for Britain and France would be necessary because Mexican nationals need them, and then, yet *another* United States tourist visa must be issued to ensure her entry back into the United States. Unbelievably stupid, complex and arcane.

And the seventh step, perhaps the most difficult step of all: once she returned to the United States after the European trip, she must obtain a legal working visa so she could continue to attend Sandy Golden. That was not like falling off a log. That took time, and I had no clue how to do it.

But the last step was too far into the future to even consider how to attempt it, and if I thought about it *too* much, it might jeopardize my enthusiasm for leaping the first six hurdles. So I drew the magical number 7 in the sand. The process required *at least* that many steps. Each one had to be executed flawlessly. A flock of sea birds flew by, racketing mercilessly, as though they were laughing at this human folly. I ran back down the beach toward my car, counting on the tide as an eraser.

The first step proved deceptively simple. On the following Monday, I filed a Petition for Annulment in Contra Costa County, served it on Tuesday, on the putative husband Scales, in custody in Lompoc Federal Prison, with an acknowledgement, an acceptance, and a certificate of incontestability, and got my friendly judge to specially set a hearing for the following Friday. It was in Scales' best interest to cooperate and sign. One less felony with which *he* could be charged. Golden sent an actress from one of his sitcoms to play Nelia; the Judge cast one rather lecherous eye on the actress, and another doubtful one on me but signed the decree. No one picked up on the fact that the pink-skinned actress was not the black-as-coal nanny.

By the following Monday, I'd made an appointment with the United States Attorney's Office in Los Angeles, provided a young, tentative deputy with a certified copy of the decree of annulment in favor of Nelia and demanded that the *United States of America v. Nelia Doe* be dismissed. I was given conditional approval of this: the young man would 'check with his boss.' Nothing happens quickly in the federal bureaucracy, and the Department of Justice was not about to give Nelia a get-out-of-jail-free card. Simply stated, there would be no document that could be presented to Nelia, once found, guaranteeing the federal case would be dismissed.

Between that Monday and Friday I busied myself performing the third step, trying to obtain a Belizean passport, and learned, to my horror, the so-called Embassy of Belize in Washington, D.C., did not issue passports to Belizean nationals in the United States because "none of them are legally here." So what to do? Well, if she were truly in Mexico, perhaps I could pay a *mordida* to some hack in Mexico City and obtain a Mexican passport. I had no idea as to the probability of this, or the risks involved. But I could not begin to do this without locating her.

A visit to the notorious Coy 'Cadillac' Coffin in Carmel Valley was in order. Coy was my old classmate and co-conspirator from our liberal arts boarding school. Might as well introduce the swashbuckler that everyone called 'Heisenberg' into this *mirepoix*, kill a few black swans for sport. It would be good catching up with the olden debbil.

CHAPTER VII

EN EL GRANDE DESIERTO

You might be asking: why is this a *saga*, and not an *epic*? During my research at the UCLA library I found that Epics are born around glowing campfires; sung by itinerant poets to the accompaniment of a lyre or fiddle; then memorized, augmented, amplified, and in due course cast in the current concrete, since the method of entertainment which originally gave them birth has become *passé*. And they are typically about human conflict or the lost leaders of such conflicts. The *Odyssey* comes to mind. Sagas, on the other hand, are picaresque adventures concerning, generally, the migration of peoples. Exodus is a saga. Sagas are familial, and can be handed down from generation to generation, like locks of hair in reliquaries. Every *campesino* illegal alien who has left his or her nest-like pueblo for the United States, every hopeful who left the culture of *mañana* for a military-industrial complex fueled on fast food, is the hero or heroine of a saga. And all the sagas and epics that ever were, and the bad movies made about them, can now be contained in a few grains of sand. They call them chips, perhaps in honor of the toxic crisps they emulate.

It's a long journey from Belize City to Sonoita, Sonora, Mexico; of that, you should have no doubt. I calculate it as three thousand kilometers, and not as the crow flies; so you had better skip this episode if you are squeamish, or beginning to think that long journeys are short paths to heaven.

My pilgrimage to the land of the brave and the home of the free started in a *panga* piloted by one of the boys from Ambergris Caye to Chetumal within the border of Mexico, where the little bloke landed me on the bank of an irrigation ditch, so I wouldn't have to pay off the border guards at Santa

Elena. From Chetumal, a place of Mayan ruins, I took a smelly bus with the dregs of those Mayan afterlife people and their green bananas across Yucatan Peninsula to Villa Hermosa; from Villa Hermosa I bought an airplane ticket to Mexico City, and then another to Hermosillo. I wanted to take the bus from Mexico City north through Chihuahua, Chihuahua, the home of Pancho Villa, and research my ancestors, but I hadn't the time, the money, or any *coyote* connection.

One didn't need a passport or driver's license or anything like that in order to fly in Mexico. One took one's life in one's hands on those old creaking Mexican planes; no *terrorista* has ever tried to hijack one. And though I slept on the bus, there was no rest on the airplanes with their whirring propellers and vibrating wings. The plane ride felt like an iguana writhing in the beak of a giant condor composed of aluminum foil.

But it was in Hermosillo where the real adventure began. This falsely pretty town, in the Sonoran desert, gives no hint as to the dangers which lie to the north. I had brought with me a backpack with few clothes, some good walking shoes, an ab iron, a sharp clasp knife, and a large supply of water. I had saved over $2000.00 in tips which would be used for my bus fare, air fare, and paying off the *coyotes* who would guide me across the *Camino del Diablo,* the so-called 'Devil's Highway', in the Northern Sonoran desert. My trip was timed during the spring, when it should not be too hot to cross, nor would we encounter the *chubascos* of winter, which might drown you in a flash flood while crossing a dry arroyo.

I had learned the rules of border jumping from a Mexicana owner of a travel agency in Belize City, purchased with her combined earnings as a *puta* in Nogales, and then, after her looks ran away, as a maid for a family in San Diego. I bought the air tickets from her. She crossed illegally in 1970, and suggested a route with the least chance of being caught by the United States *federales*: a point on the border west of a town called Sonoita. From Hermosillo I boarded a bus north on Mexican route 15 until it crossed Mexican Route 2, which flows along the border westward like a *culebra*. The town of Sonoita is but a scale on one of its coils.

On this leg of the trip, I saw amazing plants, saguaro cacti, which, like revolutionaries, thrust their twisted limbs into the sky.

Twin cemeteries embrace the approach to Sonoita. You can tell you are no longer in Honduras from the food the ragged people carry on the buses: *camotes,* candied yams, stacks of tortillas, *nopalitos,* and the occasional goat with a few hours left to live. The Mexicana told me to find a rooming house called *La Casa de Los Huespuedes*, which she described as a meeting place for border jumpers and *coyotes*.

I had trouble finding this ramshackle building because the locals knew it by another name. At this point, you must learn border vocabulary words, for I will use them to describe what happened to me next: *mordidas*, little bites, are bribes; *coyotes* are *polleros,* or chicken wranglers, which makes their clients chickens, or *pollos. Chichornias* are boobs. United States Border Patrol agents, *la migra,* or *pinche migra,* call illegals 'tonks' or 'wets', though there isn't a drop of water in Sonoita. When I stepped off the bus, the temperature could have roasted Johnnycakes. At the rooming house, I awakened a fat, evil-looking bloke with a golden tooth, sleeping and farting in a hammock. He regarded me with great suspicion, asking was I a *pollo*, which in Belize would be a male whore. I almost smacked him. Then it came to me I was dressed like a male whore.

"If you are a *pollo,* first go to the hotel." When I didn't leave, he requested *la mordida*; I told him in Spanish to go straight to hell. Then he asked, "You must be looking for '*Los Testiculos De Jehovah'* (the balls of God)," and began laughing. I had no idea of his meaning.

He continued to stare at me; I caught him looking at my *chi-chis*, not easily disguised, and with a knowing look said, "The *cantina de chichornias* is across the way."

There are traditional steps in the death waltz between the *pollos and polleros;* you first need to check into the local hotel, and from there be recruited. So I found the hotel, the San Antonio, and waited for sinful characters with blue hair, tattoos of scorpions, or other evil mackerel markings, to show up.

The Mexicana had provided me with nicknames of the various *guias*, guides, for that is how the *polleros* describe themselves: Don Moi, El Chespiro, El Negro, El Moreno, Rooster Boy, and the like. The woman who managed the San Antonio treated me as no one special, told me to appear in the lobby at 6:00 p.m. if I needed travel arrangements. Behind her on the wall a sign read:

> *"Fuck La Migra*
> *and the policia!*
> *Fuck John Wayne!*
> *I look up to Pancho Villa"*

I had landed in the right place: the *gallinero,* the chicken coop.

Pollos travel at night across the Devil's Highway in order to avoid the heat and escape detection from the *federales*. Since the path is through the desert, most of the wildlife is nocturnal, nasty, and scuttles around looking for prey: the sidewinder, the scorpion, the giant centipede, the black widow, the tarantula, the brown recluse spider, the coral snake, and the Gila monster. The kissing bug, or *chupasangre,* sucks blood and leaves a trail of feces in the bite, which makes the entire body erupt in red welts. Fungus is carried in the valley dust, and it migrates into the lungs and blossoms to life. I knew nothing about these things when entering Sonoita. Later, when trying to make sense of some of the things which had happened on my journey, I read, in the library at UCLA, this strange poem:

> *Some fungi produce mycosis*
> *like blasto or hysto plasmosis,*
> *but for musical sake*
> *the one I will take*
> *is coccidiodomycosis.*

Then there are the plants: the *chollas*, with barbed spines, which hook into and tear the skin, and the mesquite, adorned by nature with thorns intended to puncture the eye.

I should also mention the mythical creatures which are said to inhabit the nocturnal desert, such as the *Surem*, tiny men which live underground and bite your feet, *La Llorona*, a wailing ghost which rushes down the creek beds like a flash flood, various witches, and the *chupacabra*, or Goat Sucker (not to be confused with the *chupasangre*) which also siphons human blood. I knew nothing, about these, either.

I waited in the lobby to be discovered.

Looking back, it is 'ironic' (a word which has nothing to do with knives or spears), that El Chollo was the name of the first *pollero* who sidled over to me in the lobby. He had skin black as the bark of the spiky cactus of the same name, and pockmarks on his face could have been carved by its spines. A moustache dripped from his jaws like whiskers of a catfish. He told me he would need $2000.00 to 'escort' me across the border. It could be paid in pesos, and must be paid in advance. He would guide me personally, he bragged, as though traveling with him would be some sort of privilege. I told him that I would give him $1000.00, and the rest when I had safely made it to a bus station on Highway 8, beyond the claws of *la migra.* We were both fooling each other. I did not have the rest of the money. His ready acceptance of these terms made me suspicious.

He told me to check into the rooming house and be

patient. There would be a group of eleven of us crossing, four women and seven men; I must wait for them to assemble. They were not all pathetic creatures of the sort one reads about in newspaper stories. One of the girls had been a hairdresser in Vera Cruz, her shining long hair done in braids for her adventure north. Two women were older, hard, dour, fat, and uneducated. The men were young, shy, nervously joking with each other, wearing the *bracero* uniform of blue jeans, boots, and Resistol cowboy hats. I towered a foot above most of them, and they regarded me with curiosity. They must have concluded from my accent that I was not Mexican, though I told them I had been working in a bar in Mexico City. On the day, El Chollo led us from the hotel. They carried small packs, not unlike my own, stuffed with minimal possessions. A battered Coca-Cola thermometer read 92° at 9:00 a.m. on the day we departed, a Sunday.

After El Chollo negotiated with one of the bus drivers of the Pacifico Line, we boarded and were of course required to pay 50 pesos extra for the ride. The necessity of this bus trip became clear when we encountered a checkpoint of dusty Mexican army troops bearing automatic weapons, who boarded and sifted through our belongings. They must have been looking for drugs, but, fully aware we intended to escape across the border, were not going to help *la migra* by molesting us. We were important cogs in the wheels of the local economy. They let us pass; we continued westward on the road, slinking along the United States border. After only a few kilometers, El Chollo directed the bus driver to stop and we disembarked on the roadside in the middle of the desert. We were told nothing about our route or destination. We crossed an arroyo and saw our first collection of rattlesnakes, arranged like questions marks under the mesquite, dormant in the heat of the day. Soon we stepped over a collapsed barbed-wire fence. We had entered the United States of America.

I carried two extra things the others did not: a compass,

and a good map of the southern portion of the United States. The travel agent had tried to draw guideposts on it, useful things such as *tinajas,* water holes, but I didn't rely on her memory. I knew precisely where we were and where we had to go. El Chollo said, "Relax, we will wait for the ride." What ride? We slinked beneath creosote bushes to avoid helicopters and the direct rays of the sun, like scared rabbits avoiding hawks. A battered white van finally emerged on the horizon, kicking up a rooster tail of sand. We crowded into the back of this pressure cooker like parsnips. We did not proceed north, but *back* along the border toward Sonoita, in a zigzag random pattern that implied *la migra* in pursuit. I asked El Chollo why we were headed the same way we had just come. He said, "To find the pass between the mountains." I assumed he meant the pass between the Granite and Growler ranges, which bordered, on the west and east of the Devil's Highway. By this time, it was 1:45 p.m. and the heat must have been 10° more than when we left Sonoita. The driver refused to lower the van's black tinted windows, increasing the internal temperature; the Mexicans drained bottles of warm plum soda, purchased before boarding the bus at Sonoita; I just 'toughed it out'. El Chollo said we would walk at night, that it was just a matter of hours until we reached the pickup spot, from where we would be driven to Interstate 8. I knew this could not be true, unless the pickup spot was only twenty kilometers or less away. I asked him how many kilometers until the pickup spot. "*No se,*" he snarled, "but within sight of the lights of Ajo." He was growing tired of my questions, knowing his answers were stupid lies; my map showed that Ajo, which means garlic, was below the eastern flank of the Growler Mountains, named for the population of mountain lions that roamed their *barrancas.* We were going to cross them *at night*? Why, then, had we been deposited at the pass? My suspicion of El Chollo increased. By my calculations, Interstate 8 was at least eighty kilometers away when the van let us off.

After walking for an hour or so, we arrived at a large rock and were told to wait in its shadow until sunset, at which time we would begin our trek. The Mexicans, relying on El Chollo's time estimate, began guzzling water to counteract the sugar in their plum sodas. Bloody fools. I took a few sips from one of my bottles of water and tried to meditate like Gandhi.

At sunset, we padded forth into the desert. The heat, even at this time of the day, must still have exceeded 100°. At 10:00 p.m. we veered east, onto terrain which might be the Growler Mountains. Perhaps El Chollo had not lied after all; perhaps we would soon cross the summit and see the lights of Ajo. The arroyos of these foothills are treacherous; one of the women, lagging behind, was bitten by something and collapsed in the middle of a wash. No one approached her as she cursed and howled in pain. I finally cut away her chinos to examine the ankle, which had swollen to the size of a *pelota* white girls use in baseball. El Chollo provided no first aid kit, but I had been trained by my Papa how to deal with poisonous snake-bites in Belize. One cuts an X across the wound, sucks the poison, spits. I had no idea whether the woman had suffered the bite of a snake, spider, or something else, but her screaming, crying, fighting, leg kicking, objecting, and Spanish insults, made my cuts go deeper than intended, and she began to bleed heavily, which was good.

She screamed, more terrified by the blood than by the bite. I fashioned a tourniquet from one sleeve of a sweatshirt in my pack and tightened it just below the knee, and after a reasonable time bound up the wound with the other. I did not attempt to suck out the poison, because the flow of blood should have been sufficient, I assumed, to remove a great deal of it from her system. I was not going to put my mouth on this *puta*.

I won no favor among the group for my good deed; these were simple people who had never met a situation like this, nor a creature like me, and looking back, must have thought me one of the desert witches of which they had been warned. None of them came to my aid or offered words of encouragement. El Chollo sat on a boulder, brooding; I could not read his expression in the gloom, but he seemed to be contemplating his next move.

Without warning, he drew a pistol from his pack and pointed it at me through the beam of his flashlight. I studied this weapon to determine the number of bullets in the clip. He would need eleven of them to kill us all, and there was no doubt he had led us into these arroyos to do just that.

I was seated on the sand probably three meters from him. The others lay about in various postures of exhaustion. He fired the weapon into the air to establish authority and snarled, *"Cabroncitos, morros:* take *all* your *dinero* and put it in a pile in front of you. Then, put your hands at the back of your neck like this," and he demonstrated the position.

He thought I had at least an additional $1,000.00 on me, but in fact, I had just a few dollars and made no move to remove them from a money belt wrapped around my calf. The belt was concealed beneath heavy denims. But the others, in rapid succession, complied. I kept my hands high above my head but unclasped, as do victims in western movie stagecoach robberies. He collected the money in a plastic grocery bag, careful not to turn his back on any one of us, and finally approached me. "Well, what about it?" he demanded, brandishing the weapon. I lowered one arm as if to comply, pulling up my pant leg to reveal the money belt, while I grabbed the handle of the ab iron and drew it from my pack with the other. He leaned forward when he saw the belt. I grabbed a handful of sand and threw it in his face, at the same time bringing the ab iron crashing down on his head. I found out an ab iron is deadly when applied to a human skull, splitting his into two segments. His knees buckled and his brains spilled on the sand like shiny papaya seeds, caught in the light of a new moon, peering with curiosity over the lip of the arroyo. I felt as high as the first time Esmé's father entered me. I grabbed both the *cabron's* flashlight and weapon and emptied the contents of the bag onto the sand.

"Here," I said to my fellow travelers, "come get your money."

Their reaction to the events of the last several minutes amazed me. After realizing the man who would murder them had just died, they lamented, wailing they were now lost in the desert without a guide, that they would all die, and I was the one responsible for their plight. Their investment in the *coyote* had not paid off. They wailed and gnashed their teeth like a lost Biblical tribe, but made no move toward the pile of money, which had become, to them, irrelevant.

It was now 2:00 a.m. My fellow companions gathered in two groups, discussing in low voices what to do. I did not join in their gossip. The bitten woman continued to moan, and eventually fell asleep. The others followed suit. I climbed from the arroyo to the top of a large smooth boulder, which would be difficult for rattlesnakes, bugs, and anything else lurking in the darkness to mount.

This rock was also a respectable distance from the corpse of El Chollo. I had never killed anyone before (though I had thought about it), and wondered if the bloke was entitled to a proper burial. The accusatory moonlight kept me awake. Is moonlight supposed to make one feel guilty? I had brained my share of fish, some almost as large as El Chollo, but, unlike him, I treated them nobly, and did not waste their flesh. I had good feelings about killing this . . . this . . . biped. And I figured that the vultures we had seen in great numbers the previous day would make short work of him in the morning, and that this should be the natural order of things.

During the night, helicopters, toys of *la migra,* whined overhead. Their searchlights did not pierce the arroyos of the

Growler Range, but searched the flat plain below for prospective captives. This confirmed my suspicion we had not followed the usual track.

I told the bright moon to go straight to hell but still got no sleep. At daybreak, I heard a weird whining and yelling. I peered down into the arroyo and saw the group watching a pack of El Chollo's namesakes dismembering him. My companions yelled as though watching a bullfight, as a coyote would rip off a piece of his flesh. I thought of scattering the pack with his pistol but decided not to interfere with the course of nature. Dollar bills and pesos flew out of El Chollo's pants as the coyotes ripped him to shreds.

When the group saw me standing on the rock, several of the young men shook their fists at me; the bitten woman was still alive, so I could not have done her much harm. The group exhibited more courage in the daylight; they signified they would continue eastward, over the mountains, in the direction they thought would lead them to Ajo. When they got there, they said, they would report me to the authorities for killing their countryman. Not bloody likely. If they continued in the direction the *coyote* laid out, they would meet only their Maker.

I was happy when they took their leave. I then retraced our steps of the previous evening. This was not difficult because ours were the only footprints – no breeze had arisen to erase the sands. I walked westward and concluded that marching through this desert during the day was not much warmer than at night and significantly safer, though perhaps more obvious to *la migra*. I wore a New York Yankees ball cap, of minimal use in disguising me as Mexican male. Since I no longer needed my shirt, I poured water on it, tied it around my head, replaced the cap, and made a sort of primitive air conditioner. I came to the center of the featureless plain between both set of mountains and turned due north. Looking at the map, I knew the further I travelled in this direction the sooner I would encounter Interstate 8, at a place called, strangely, Dateland.

After fourteen hours of walking, and draining three bottles of water, at about 4:00 a.m. I saw the lights, not of a city, but a closed *bodega* that advertised, "Home of the Date Shake." So a 'date' in this context was not an occasion to make *bam bam*, but some class of food.

I crossed a railroad track. A good sign. There was a trailer park next to the *bodega*, but no motel. I slipped through the door of a metal shed alongside the tracks, thinking there might be some hay to hide in. Instead, it was filled with cardboard barrels filled with what Belizeans would call monkey shit. I nibbled at one of the shriveled pellets, which in the glare of my flashlight appeared truly disgusting. They were sweet, dry, and stuck in my teeth, as wicked bad to taste as to view. If you encountered one in your bedclothes, you might conclude your plumbing had gone to rot.

So I just lay on the concrete floor among these barrels, hidden, and, using my pack as a pillow, fell asleep.

When I awakened at 10:00 a.m., the sky was again a perfect blue, and a train had arrived on the siding next to the tin hut, perhaps to collect the barrels. What did American people *do* with these nasty pellets? No matter. The train was headed west, and that was where I wanted to go. I crawled under a tarp lashed to a flatcar carrying tubs of something labeled 'chlorine'. And since I knew that it was used, among other things, to purify the water in swimming pools, I thought that if I just stuck with it long enough, it might lead me to a job. It has always amazed me how seemingly unrelated coincidences lead one forward, like railroad ties, diminishing into the distance toward an uncertain point.

CHAPTER VIII

IN THE PEACH TRAILER

Whoa, dudes, haul galoties and lissen up: enter into the world of Coy Coffin. Shane calls me Coy 'Cadillac' Coffin because of my subterranean 1956, Candy Apple Red El Dorado convertible, buried in the sand behind my kip. Well, it ain't buried yet, folks. Not like Yucca Mountain. So I have forty acres or so more or less southeast of Yermo, named for Gills Yermo, the famous sturgeon fisherman. Very little caviar in this neck of the woods, 'ceptin what you produce yourself. More on that later.

So on this one particular morning, I believe it was in May of 1984, Himself, the not-so-prominent lawyer of the Hopeless and the Damned, comes trudgin' 'cross the desert sands toward what old Joseph P. Kennedy would have called a 'compound'. What a sight for my sore eyes on a hung-over Sunday morning! Visible through the magic eye of one of a dozen security cameras scanning from the roof of my Airstream. As usual, he had one of his so-called paralegals in tow. Surprisingly, she wasn't a tall blond on high heels tottering in the sand, but a little Mexicana about the size of Dopey in *Snow White*. Have you ever heard my joke about what happens to Snow White when she goes to heaven? Probably not. Shane *y yo* were once roommates in a little liberal arts college, which for criminal law reasons must remain anonymous. Damn, when Shane cut out for wiles of Berkeley it was never the same. Who else would help steal an F-15 negligently left in the student quadrangle to induce all of us liberal artists to bomb geeks in Phweet Blam? I mean *gooks*. Well, maybe all the poor bombed out gooks have now become geeks. We hoisted that damned war machine off its jacks, and rolled it down into beautiful Lake LaSalle, where we covered it with toilet paper, leaving visible only the 'R' and the 'F'. You know what that means, right?

The San Francisco *Chronicle* came out and took a picture of it. Damn, I wish I had one of those. Then the FBI arrived, and Shane hid in the dumb waiter between the cafeteria and the infirmary. Old toothless Liz, the nurse, stopped it mid-floor. She loved Shane-O, fetched him up in that dumb waiter to administer a blow job or two. FBI thought it was a rat-fuck in any event – no sane person loved the war in Southeast Asia.

I remember one time Shane intervened before I knocked the block off some asshole who said something nasty about my then girlfriend's boobs. He suddenly accused him of being a *fenestrator*. That diverted the son-of-a-bitch, all right. Well, *he* had never fenestrated! "By the way Shane, what *is* fenestration?"

"A perversion of the third orifice," Shane claimed.

"Huh?????"

"Shit, ask your minister," sez old Shane, in disgust. He defined his own moments: saved that buckwheat some broken teeth. So when he fled for Berkeley we missed him. He *had* to have a Berkeley degree, you dig, one from our little college wouldn't do. Had to have it. Christ, in those days he thought he was Lord Byron – needed his sleep on avocado green sheets, or the plug would be pulled on his power, like cutting Samson's hair, or somethin'. Byron had a coach built which copied Napoleon's, didja know? Well, Shane drove[2] an old Mercedes Benz convertible with suicide doors, which must have been owned by Himmler.

'Cause he had been bitched since his natural (?) father tried to cut his leg off with a carving knife like in the nursery

---

[2] Not strictly true, in that its generator was busted. We had to push the damn thing to get it started.

rhyme. I paid big bucks to various off campus shrinks to set him straight. It would have been boring if he turned out as some linear guy. We once set fire to the speed bumps on the entrance road of our college to keep the shocks in my 'Vette and his staff car from getting bruised. But that is another story from a magical time.

To let him in I clicked open the electric lock on the hurricane fence gate, topped with coiled razor sharp barbed wire. Then he had to navigate the forest of *cardones*, dark Baja born sentinels which can rip you apart easier than the barbed wire. I barked some commands through the loud speaker to calm the *canis caneris*, who would have been happy to sink his teeth in the dark meat of that Hispanic chick. Saw Shane lookin' suspicious-like at my clothes a molderin' in the fire ring. The long horned yellow-eyed Angora goats paid no attention to this pair. They just kept munchin' away in the truck garden to the left of the Airstream. I have one hell of an organic garden, including politically correct arugula and green kale. If this country started eatin' endive, we could probably elect a Tibetan president.

To the right of the trailer is the cactus arboretum: I paid nary a dime for these succulents[3], just visited ol' Billy Wrigley's botanical garden on Santa Catalina and took clippings from hundreds of species he scrounged from various exotic climes. My childless uncle left me millions from his insurance racket when he kicked in Chicago, and that very moment I got rid of my Gant shirts with their little loops sewn into the back, and U-turned back into myself. What I'm sayin'? I don't need none of your jack, Jack.

So, from the Feds point of view, though the *canis caneris* might well signify a crack lab, I appear as a goat farmer and

---

[3] Don't you just *love* how that word sounds?

an organic environmentalist.

Now, in the back of the trailer, well out of sight, is a pit which holds my old Caddy, top down. An aluminum shed protects it from the sun, and I've got a little gunga din who does nothing but polish it and treat the white leather interior. Around the pit are massive volcanic boulders, and a D-cat for pushin' 'em in. The radio used to be set to oldies but goodies, but the station faded out, like everything else seems to these days; so I put in a tape deck with the Grateful Dead Singing *Touch of Gray*. If you have ever skied, at least when I used to ski, every damned lift operator in the country had the Grateful Dead playing, and often that very song. In any event, when my mortal coil uncoils, I will be placed in the driver's seat and gunga din will D-cat in 'dem boulders. It is my pyramid, my starship. Not that I believe in an afterlife. I don't much care the destination; carmick cruise control will decide. But I know that when space aliens eventually explore the burnt out earth, they will dig this thing up and totally misrepresent what was going on here; to fool countless generations of unidimensional idiots. Kinda like in Kubrick's *2001: A Space Odyssey*. Kubrick thought we might be a lot further along than we turned out to be, dig? Dig. I *do not* relish the thought of being exhumed; no postmortem blood or DNA testing, drug indictments, or clambering Jeffersonian offsprings from paternity suits.

That certain morning when Shane decided to appear, my aching bones were splayed on a cast iron Victorian trundle aqua bed, the side of my face pressed upside the bars. He finally came waltzing through the door with the *mamacita*.

She wore a dark blue skirt well below the knee, (and, let me tell you, there wasn't much going on between the knee and the ankle) a white blouse with a Peter Pan collar of the type you still can buy in certain Jaycee Pennae stores in Mississippi, a gold crucifix danglin' from a chain about her neck, *nylons,* and sensible black shoes of the type nuns wore

in the fifties. You can be sure that was the first time the dyin'
Christ, or the Christ in any guise, darkened my door.

Her brown eyes, framed in a round face beneath curly
black hair, grew to *empanada* size when she got a look at me.

"I hope you brought me some clothes. A G-string,
anything . . ." I said by way of greeting.

I was buck nekkid.

"What the fuck happened to you? You look like Wallace
the Lion after he swallowed Albert."

"Some Jewish bitch. A geologist. With a little silver pick
ax. Comes grubbin' along and I like a fool let her in. She
played post-coital possum with me. When she's sure I'm
asleep, grabs all my clothes, torches 'em in the charcoal pit
in front."

"What the hell rang *her* chimes?"

I'm sure Shane could imagine the answer to this, but
wanted to force a confession from my poor chapped lips.

"After she gave me a 9.2 scale head, I told her, the reason
Hebe babes are *pre-eminent* blow job artists (this was
intended as a compliment) is due to the genetic drive to
produce a superior race, like Hitler. First, they clean you out
with maximum suction, so what's left is a jolt of the best and
brightest – I used Monica Lewinsky as an example – but *this*
chick saved cum in her throat, then hocked a giant loogie into
the toilet, as though she had chugged arsenic."

(Oh, excuse *me* Mother Cabrini.)

"More info than I needed to know," said Shane, "but
charred U-trou? Reminds one of the Nazi book burning all
right. You need to be careful. 'Where they burn books, they
also burn people.' Thus spoke Heinrich Heine. This young
lady is Alicia, my paralegal."

"Heine," I snorted, "up *your* hiney, Shane. Greetings, Alicia."

Alicia gave a little bow, which did not alter her look of shock.

Shane threw a pair of shorts and a t-shirt at me. Gentleman to the core, I pulled them on under the covers.

"She could have torched the Peach Trailer," said Shane, as he ran his hands (reminiscing, I think) along the laminate interior of my ancient Airstream, its walls paneled in vertically pin-striped mahogany, like the deck of an old Chris Craft Runabout. Come to think of it, the Airstream is of that vintage. In one corner, a stainless steel partition of quilted sheet metal defines a kitchen or, more accurately, a lab. My real business? I am the master brewer of I-Brau, man. The only carbonated peyote beverage available on any market, let alone the *black*. One day, for fun, I threw some peyote buttons in a kettle, and the rest is history. Soon, a greenish mist made for rough landings in the old Airstream, but when I woke up several days later, there was this white precipitate on the walls. I scraped it off with a squeegee, combined it with a little watercress and soda water, and *voila*. So what you see behind the quilted sheet metal is a still, and it doesn't take much whoopee juice to make *gallons* of I-Brau.

A lot of people do their best thinking while sucking this stuff down; it creates a kind of Carlos Castaneda out of body experience. Little Billy Gates and Steve Jobs are both good customers. There is a less popular snack food sold in little cans: you can snort pinches of the powder at your leisure, like a baseball pitcher inhales snuff. In fact, that longhaired hippy dude who hurls for the Giants stopped throwin' curves when he went offen it.

"My friend Coy here is quite the inventor," Shane said to Alicia (nervous like, as though he was 'shamed of me.) "He concocts this medicine which almost makes the living rise from the dead. It's a type of painkiller. Fully licensed, of course." Alicia nodded her head gravely.

"Hey, d'ya want some green eggs 'n *nopalitos*?" I said.

"I've already had my breakfast, thank you, Sir," she said quickly, hands clasped in lap.

So I have these wild Peruvian hens, which eat the goat *ca ca* and produce delph blue eggs, shells like Limoges, yolks the color of the sunset over Negril. Been thinkin' of sellin' 'em under the mark Holy Organics. I'm also a gourmet cook, adept at concealing poisons. These, with other less toxic plants, grow like hell behind my chain-linked fence.

"Coy, you can slap an omelet upside my head, but focus, Laddo, we got some serious work to do here. I tried to call you, your phone must be disconnected."

"Those cock-sucking AT&T monopolistic bastards cut off my cellphone. 'Cause they kept calling and I told them to fuck off. But I fixed 'em: when I went in to pay my bill, I forwarded my phone number to their corporate offices in New York. It will be like a dog chewin' on its own dick, 'cause they got to call before they can cut you."

"OK. Here's the gig – do you remember that Mexican *chica* you were dating from Chihuahua, Ofelia, or Lobelia, something like that?"

"Olelia. O-le-li-a *Habanera* you mean. How could I forget her? What do you want with her? I love the way her name sloshes around my gums. *Una perra peligrosa,* little brother. *Una perra* muy *peligrosa.*"

"I represent a damsel in distress. More like, a nanny in need. She is *stateless,* Coy, hasn't a passport nor green card, *nada*. Entered illegally. And she is *missing*. My paralegal Alicia here has agreed to adopt her; because Mexican law says at least then we can get her a Mexican passport. Alicia still has Mexican citizenship, but comes from Toluca. *La*

Habanera has got connections in Chihuahua, right? We think my client might be hiding out there. D'ya think *La Habanera* can whip up an adoption decree and a birth certificate? Quickly? As in, create an adoption certificate that will work in the Department of Foreign affairs in Mexico City to get a passport? She's a nanny. Can't tell you the real client's name. But 100 large says you can help."

Now *this* was truly unusual; it was clear the only thing Shane was getting from the dwarf was legal advice – but money? He had gotten a client with *money?* He usually represented the unwashed, unentitled, and impoverished. But I had to warn him of whatever danger was sure to accompany his Quixotic legal recipes. He never seemed to pay much attention to it, when on a roll.

"Why is she missing?"

"Too complex . . . we *think* she ran off to Mexico. To Chihuahua."

"Well, the trip with Olelia is that you never know who she's really working for when she's supposed to be working for you. She will change sides for a price, 'as quick as a rabbit gets fucked', to paraphrase Al Pacino. When she was fucking me, I could always tell by her eyes that, in her imagination, she was doing someone else – out of *something.* She runs on money, sex, and sometimes death, in that order."

"It's really all about the passport, whether you can organize the Chihuahua side, whether you want to help with this or not, and if you don't trust *La Habanera* or whomever, you use someone else. Coy! It's a ten grand merit badge: that's my authority, that's my budget."

Hell, this presented as a nothin' problem. For fat commissions, I do things for Gringos legal in Mexico but illegal in the United States, such as, pick up a kidney in Zacatecas for shipment to Hong Kong. One of my pet projects is to light the world without pollution, by bioluminescent algae. Bob Redford at Sundance has on his desk a movie, which just shows some bioluminescent footprints dancing in the sand.

I just scratched my head and yawned. No particular risk here.

"It's not going to be so easy locating *La Habanera*. Where the hell she hangs out now is anyone's guess."

I decided to tweak Shane: "So you're still in the business of shitting paper for paperwork. You bring darkness into the world, I try for light. We both do rock on, lil' bro, do we not? Lay that $10K on me. I'll start trying to find her. *Fiat tenebrae.*"

CHAPTER IX

ESMÉ SQUALOR

For an infant with incomplete use of her legs, a home on stilts was both elevating and depressing. Esmé first learned to crawl around the sparse bamboo furniture while staring at the dust motes filtering through latticed windows. She could then pull herself up on the sill by a pair of strong arms so she could see what she imagined were bubbles drifting across the blue sky. She made friends with the stars that penetrated the night, counted them to sleep. She corralled various insects who inhabited the floor, but, unlike other infants, did not try to consume them. They were her toys, her unsuccessfully colonized lead soldiers. She often tried to make a bridge of her body but collapsed on the floor; this continuing effort to use muscles in her legs made them shapely. As she grew older, she wondered why a woman's most beautiful curves lead to such dead ends. Her arms became levers, catapults, stanchions – she learned to fly up and down the rope ladder Mama made her which could be lowered from a trap door in a corner of the dwelling. She avoided the hardwood stairs and their splinters.

Mama also crafted heavy corduroy overalls for crawling and climbing, and tied a rope to a branch over the Macal for swinging. Esmé welcomed the overalls; she did not miss the way the rough hemp of the rope chafed the skin between her legs. Her long hair, uncut and untended, fell across her back like a tangled fishing net. Like her Mama, she became an expert swimmer and *pescadera,* with both harpoon and line.

Her skin was cocoa butter in color, and her eyes aquamarine. She learned early on to control her playmates and physical environment with those eyes. She was Draconian. She made a small cage of bamboo imprisoning one of her lead soldiers, a cricket, as punishment for shattering the night stillness.

She thought he made the stars tremble by shaking his reggae marimba legs. Then she practiced hypnotizing him with one laser glance penetrating *his* pixilated stare. She fed him ripe watermelon and dust motes, the smallest infantrymen in her insect army.

The chirping of the cricket meant bedtime, his silence, dawn. No primer need teach her monthly cycles; the moon informed her when Mama would arrive from somewhere far away; she learned many other children in the province of Cayo had absent or missing fathers, and as soon as she learned to speak, at eighteen months, her first phrases were '*mama va*' and '*hombre se fue*'.

Mama would always leave books (Spanish on one page, English translation the next) scattered on the floor; Esmé poured over the symbols she thought might decode mysteries in the dust motes, the canopy of stars, the pixels in the cricket's eyes. Mama's touch was like velvet fire, her voice, when singing folk songs, allowed Esmé's imagination to hover, like a *mariposa*, over the town. She could see the calico prints of family plots of maize, squash, and strawberries grown for the market in Belize City, and watch the Macal twist its copper body through the mangroves and palms. Another book showed pictures of a little prince riding a magic carpet through the stars. For a short while, she became the *bruja* of San Ignacio. She and Mama fit the white witch more than the princess paradigm.

But Mama vanished, the songs ceased, the magic tokens swept from the floor by her grandpapa who believed they had transformed his virginal Nelia into a Desireé who had under the auspices of some devil forged another mouth to feed.

Esmé became acquainted with pain early on. Hypodermics. Jabbed with spikes like the teeth of the needlefish on display in Grandpapa's *pescaderia*. She never cried, but the doctor learned to avoid those deadly, five-year-old eyes. The treatments became more intense. Her legs were placed in a machine which involuntarily pumped them up and down. She heard talk between Mama and Grandpapa about lack of funds for this treatment. Then, one day in spring, Mama returned with all her belongings from the island where she worked. Mama explained that she would go north to find a job with more money; that when she found a home in which they could both safely live, she would return for her; and later, if he wanted to come, Grandpapa would join. Esmé did not cry but calmly accepted this as her fate. Her primary sustenance and comfort came, after all, from the world of her imagination, not from the world of pain.

But by the time many more full moons had elapsed between Mama's departure and the day the soldier men came waving guns at Grandpapa, shouting, and looking at her as though they were about to snatch her away – even she began to lose hope.

CHAPTER X

CHIHUAHUA

No way was my Cessna 410 going anywhere near Chihuahua, Chihuahua. Rumors abounded that *federales* in Northern Mexico planted drugs aboard American private planes while parked, seized them, and sometimes ransomed their owners as well as the plane. I wished to avoid controversy or custody. So I just flew to Phoenix on Pacific Southwest Airlines (the stewardesses had short mini-skirts and long reputations – "Good afternoon, Mr. Fitzgerald," whispered a blond honey leaning over the seat in front on the largely empty aircraft, "My name is Mary Elizabeth McDonough, but you can call me 'Tibby'. Want a cocktail?") When I landed, I rented a car. The border between Nogales and El Paso must be reconnoitered to determine the best way to smuggle Nelia *back* into the country, were she found.

Chihuahua, Chihuahua, Chihuahua: repeat it to yourself; it is comfort food for the soul and easy on the ears, like the sough of surf on a tropical shore.

The grandiose names of this town's boulevards reflect significant dates in Mexican history, such as, *Avenida de la Diez y Nueve de Janiereo,* in contrast to its detritus, garbage, and dilapidated storefronts. These names are both a source of pride for the locals, and a make-work for sign painters, printers, and map-makers. Unlike most other Mexican streets, no dogs scrounge about in the dust.

But the principal square is guarded by dozens of identically shaped statues of *canis familiaris*, the shorthaired creature for which this burg is supposedly named. Or vice-versa. Sitting on their haunches, these three foot high figurines seem to be fabricated of porcelain but probably are fiberglass, painted yellow and black like Checker cabs, fire-engine red, aquamarine, or in psychedelic colors, like John Lennon's Rolls-Royce or George's uniform in *Sergeant Pepper's Lonely Hearts Club Band*. Tourists are entrained to believe these dogs originated from this skid mark in the Northern Sonoran desert. Can you picture such hairless runts scampering around the broiling, unpopulated 'Chihuahuan' desert prior to Spanish exploration, harassed by hawks, crushed by *culebras*, and consumed by coyotes?

Like many other very interesting innovations, these dogs originated in China, were imported to Spain by traders, and exported by Spanish settlers to Mexico. They did not originate with the Aztecs. And Chihuahua is neither an Aztec nor Spanish name. The Mandarin pronunciation for this animal is 'Chiwawa' (the pinyin construction) meaning: Chinese doll. Why the place might be named for a Chinese dog is a mystery, other than, perhaps, to lure tourists, like the Hualapai's transparent horseshoe walkway suspended over the Grand Canyon, Wall's Drug Store in Grand Forks, North Dakota, or P. T. Barnum's egress. Or maybe the name came from the Apaches and is another 'coincidence.' But there are no coincidences.

Tourists who really prefer cats to dogs, and who presumably never visited China, sneaked them across the border and into the United States. Though Chihuahuas are not on the menu in Chihuahua, as they might be in, say, Guangzhou, you can't find one alive, cooked, or stuffed in its shops, restaurants, or dusty streets. Chihuahua's 'skyline', if there is such a thing, reminded me of Hemmingway's description of Paris' mansard roofs in *A Moveable Feast*. Some of the buildings were actually baroque in design.

So if you were looking for someone in Paris in the 20s, I reasoned, you would start with Pére la Chaise Cemetery and, next, check the platforms at its railway stations, beginning with Gare St. Lazare. Ask the porters if they had seen an Amazonian giantess. They remembered such things in those days. My search for Nelia, therefore, began at the local train depot. She might well have arrived by train.

At the station, I found ochre skinned Indians lounging about the platform, sporting black Prince Valiant bangs, red headbands, and white loincloths. They chewed on some sort of dried cricket, or locust. The percussive arpeggios of these *niñas de la tierra,* as sharp as the thorns on *cholla*, overlaid the base notes of a chugging and hissing outgoing train. The Indians wore Adidas, New Balance, Asics and Polo tennis shoes. They begged for coins. Had I stumbled across the set of a Western movie?

These characters were *Tarahumaras*, Indians who could run like hell through the desert, barefoot; who lived in the Mexico's Copper Canyon; who were now reduced to scrabbling for coins; and who were apparently full fed up with scorpion bites on their insteps.

The train serviced Mexico's 'Grand Canyon', connecting Chihuahua with Guaymas, an insignificant town on the Gulf of California near the pesticide infected *cloaca* of the Colorado River. In Spanish, I asked these Indians and the stationmaster if they had seen 'a tall black lady with short black hair', and displayed a photo of Nelia provided by the Goldens. Though no tracks connected Chihuahua to either Nogales or El Paso, where she might have crossed, she could have walked across at Tijuana, taken a bus to Guaymas, and the train to Chihuahua. In those days, the Mexicans did not much care who entered their country by crossing at Tijuana. The Indians muttered, *'no se'*, and turned away.

The only photo the Goldens had been able to locate of Nelia continued to trouble me. It showed a very tall woman, dressed in a maid's uniform, white tights, and white shoes, bending forward attentively. She had her face turned away from the camera toward Sandy Golden, who looked up at her with devotion: all we can see is the close-cropped hair on the back of her head. But there is something familiar, something alluring about her profile. Why had she chosen to come to Chihuahua, Chihuahua, of all places? There must be a link between it and her past. And there was something else troubling about the photograph, which was as yet undefined. I left the train station and headed downtown.

The Museum of The Mexican Revolution, located along one of Chihuahua's dusty boulevards, was once the home of Francisco 'Pancho' Villa.[4] It shares the same cracked-adobe façade with any number of Mexican restaurants in Southern California. Incidentally, there are certainly more bad restaurants in Chihuahua than dogs of that name. Even though, as you must remember, a cartoon Chihuahua serves as a mascot of an American taco chain, where other canine remnants find eternal sleep between folded tortillas.

The first thing I noted after paying a twenty peso admission fee was an old, black, Dodge sedan, set up in the foyer, riddled with blood-encrusted bullet holes. Pancho Villa met his sorry end in this vehicle. I stuck my little finger in one of the bullet holes, careful of the still sharp internal flanges. The assassins must have shot from a single venue; I could not recall the historical explanation of their motives.

I wandered through the rooms of this fascinating old hacienda; its physical trappings were those of an aristocrat, not a peasant. One room was devoted to weaponry and saddles, as in a medieval castle. Villa had a habit of using

---

[4] The only thing I really knew about Villa is that he was a '*bandido*', and that you could buy T-shirts of him (or of Chairman Mao) from the stores on Telegraph Avenue when I was at Berkeley. But what I didn't know then is that he probably offed my departed fellow member of the Peregrine Club, Ambrose Bierce, when they rode south after the Battle of Tierra Blanca in 1913. We Peregrines were cautioned by the Membership Committee to be cautious of anyone who had assassinated one of our members, but Villa was the victim of his own assassination by the time I was admitted to that privileged, eclectic group.

carved busts of his enemies, such as Benito Juarez, as saddle horns; another pommel had been fashioned from a real human skull.

"The head of a Chinaman," an attendant remarked, as though there could be no better use for Chinese skulls.

"Was Villa a Sino basher?" I murmured out loud, but the attendant just shrugged and smiled. Maybe Villa didn't cotton to the creepy imported dogs. There are certainly no images of Chinese skulls or Chihuahuas in the photographic history of the Mexican Revolution.

A trestle table of dark, highly polished wood in the middle of a small dining room had been set for dinner, as if Villa, larger than life, would charge through the door at any moment. The sterling flatware rested on little trestles supported by two six-pronged objects, which looked like the jacks so familiar to children. These were intended to prevent knives and forks from soiling linen or lace. It occurred to me that the legendary Villa, variously portrayed as a *bandido*, rogue, rapist, roué, border raider, or bloodthirsty corrupt revolutionary, could be out of place presiding over such a sophisticated table. And it raised a question in my mind as to whether Villa might have been condemned by American journalists and historians to that popular myth of *bandido* reserved for south-of-the-border leaders who chafed at Washington's puppet strings. I considered these ironies while ascending a narrow spiral staircase to a second floor loggia, an art gallery filled with cases of medallions, walls festooned with proclamations, photographs, and paintings of heroic Mexican revolutionary scenes and heroes. In the center of one wall, by itself, hung a remarkable photograph, beneath which a small altar, with blazing votive candles, had been placed. The corroded plaque on the frame of the photograph read, in Spanish, 'La Valentina, Ramirez Avitia, heroine of the Mexican Revolution.'

"*Una adelita*," said my tour guide, noticing my interest.

The photo depicts a tall young woman of between 18 and 22, wearing an open necked shirt, bandoliers stuffed with shells crisscrossing her breasts, chaps, and high riding boots. She is in the middle of a desert, somewhere, shadowed by blurred horses, *charros*, a pueblo of sorts, and lots of sand. The background is of little consequence, because the photo is dominated by the clean lines of the young woman's face. Her lynx eyes are set between high Indian cheekbones; we cannot ascertain their shade from this black and white print, but a felinity suggests they were yellow-green.

I stood transfixed before this icon for five minutes before appreciating its significance. At first, the eyes reminded me of childhood games of marbles: chase and capture played with pureys in the sand. Then I realized they were more like the green, yellow, and black-vaned cat's eyes, glassy spheres that glowed immediately after lights out in the velvet darkness of childhood. I had encountered these eyes in the photograph before, and I now remembered where.

I walked downstairs to where the attendant had retreated into his kiosk, showed him Nelia's photo, and asked: "Have you seen this lady before?"

The man chuckled and replied, "Ah, *La Negrita*. She comes every day with candles for *La Valentina*. Her relative, she says."

"At what time, usually?"

"During *siesta* time. She works at the bar of the *El Gato Negro* at night. They have great *cabrita* there," he said, winking at me. Did he mean 'goat', or 'tail'?

When I finally located this place that evening, the only sign was a black cat wood-burned in a heavy oak door. It didn't block the inevitable *Norteño* music blaring away. The German immigrants to sizzling Northern Mexico blessed the land with their recipes for beer, but cursed it with the accordion. As to cats, I considered their highest and best use burrito fillings in San Ysidro. Accordions should face Death Squads without trial.

The attractive woman behind the bar immediately recognized me as I stepped through the bricked archway of *El Gato Negro* that evening. Her short haircut made her look a little like a very tall Joan Baez, dressed in a simple black Indio shift with embroidered bodice. We locked eyes. Startled, she stopped wiping down the bar. This *couldn't* be the same girl – we had been together only once, on that evening long ago on Caya Esmeralda. She did not run from behind the bar to greet me, arms opened in welcome.

"Desireé?" I whispered, approaching the bar, "Or Nelia? How can this be?"

"What are you doing in Chihuahua, 'Mr. Inevitable'?" she managed a smile. "Long time no see." Her close-cropped hair was shiny, like a seal's.

"Your hair. I almost couldn't tell. But I remember your eyes."

"Is that *all* you remember? There is another change."

"And then?"

"We have a child."

My stomach flipped, my guts clenched. Kismet.

"Why didn't you try to reach me, to get in touch with me? I already have four children, I told you that!" This was not a wise response. I needed to chill. Fighting with former lovers is never a recipe for success.

"That has little to do with the price of tea, doesn't it? I have concluded it must be what I wanted at the time. I had no way of reaching you. You didn't come back. I didn't know your real name. I don't know it now. You don't have to tell me! I was going to name her Fatima, after the virgin, you know, that place where the Catholics believe in the apparition. But I named her Esmé Squalor, instead. I don't need you, really. Really! I support her even though she is not . . . right. How did you find me here? Why *are* you here?"

Esmé. Esmé Squalor. Not right. What would my wife have to say about this? How would it affect my duties to the Goldens? Holy good night!

"We are both in a world of deep shit, I'm afraid. I represent the Goldens. I came here to locate Nelia and found Desireé."

"You do *what*?"

"I work for the Goldens."

"So do I. I did, I mean."

"I know."

"That is why I had to run away; they have no idea of all the *pinche migra* trouble. They are so rich and spoiled they never swim in the sea of garbage below them, especially the wife, the Missy, *una bruja*. Mr. is nice, though, and I love Sandy."

I plopped on a barstool, feeling like some alien lost in a parallel universe. I buried my face in my hands. The owner of the restaurant, who had given me a casual glance, now focused on us. I threw a load of pesos on the bar to quiet him. Nelia began to swab at the counter again. There was good news, and bad news. The good news: I had found Nelia. The bad news: she was a gorgeous zombie from my past whom I had left with child – a disabled child. Literature is full of dusky bastard children difficult to explain to wives. But whitewashed siblings are, in all literature, characteristically the most unforgiving – they will inevitably side with their mother, unless she be a virago from hell.

"We don't have those fancy drinks here," said Nelia. In response to my quizzical glance, she added: *"'They're very ordinary-looking fish when they swim in, but once they get in, they behave like pigs,'"* quoting from Salinger. I had best remember every nuance of our ever-so-brief romance, or at least pretend that I did. That much was now clear.

"How is Esmé 'not right?'" I asked.

"She is afflicted with what you *gringos* call cerebral palsy. That does not make her uncherished in my eyes, though."

I remember the plummeting-elevator-sinking-soul-overripe-avocado feeling of bruised despair, with no bottom, no end. I was responsible for creating this creature of pain.

"Nelia – can I tell the Goldens that I have found you?"

"*Cho* – no way! They will want me back. I cannot go back there. No."

"I – they, I mean – can protect you."

"Poor silly man. You are still trying to lap dance on the edge of magic, isn't it? They don't know that I – that we – have a kid, and I don't want them to know. Sandy thinks I am his mother. Well, I am in a way. I don't want to return if I am going to be put in any jail. But I am sure you will do what you are trained to do, first playing at being noble, then, playing at being fearless. Playing at being one or more characters in the books you constantly read, even though I think you are deep down just a scared little man."

I remembered that California had the highest inmate-to-population ratio of any demography on the planet. I took her point. The last comment cut because it had the ring of truth. But I said:

"Sandy isn't thinking anything, Nelia. He is in a coma." That overcame any resistance, or the fear she certainly had. It was my trump card, and, thank God, it worked.

She poured me a beer. Studied me with her eyes. Turned

toward another customer. I saw the bubbles fighting each other for extinction on the surface of the glass, saw it grow cold with precipitation. Waited until I could hoist my glass without a shaking hand.

Coming into in the bar, I had seen one of those usually non-operative Mexican pay phones. I put in a call to Mandy Golden, who, after wasting about 100 pesos worth of time, finally deigned to come on the line.

I told her the good news about the discovery of Nelia. I did not tell her about my other discovery. She acted as though the good news was her personal entitlement.

"You must be a kind of genius, though, like they said. When will you bring her back? Will you bring her back tomorrow? Will you bring her back in time for the departure of the train? It is scheduled to leave Los Angeles on June 14th."

"I can't guarantee that, Missy. But it is certainly the next part of my mission. I am going to bring my paralegal, Alicia, into this now. She will assist in a number of ways."

"She will no doubt cost us more. Is she as expensive as you?"

"No. She only packs a Bible."

Missy Golden laughed, gaily, at this.

"Call us when you are scheduled to come in and we will send the limos," like the whole thing is just a cakewalk, right out of central casting. 'And don't forget the wasabe.'

'As if,' I thought, and ended the phone conference. Christ! Talk about a conflict of interest. So you leave Nelia here, right, fly back, declare the conflict of interest: 'I have a daughter by this lady and don't want to risk her imprisonment.' Clients' jaws drop. They've hired Bluebeard as their counsel. Sandy's awakening indefinitely postponed.

Return the hundred Gs. Bring in new counsel because of the fuck up. *Pay* for new counsel because of the fuckup. Alert the State Bar. Do whatever. Think again, Shane Fitzgerald, Esq. Think again!

But to Nelia I pleasantly said, "So . . . we have a daughter!"

"I have a picture, though, if you would like to see her."

Book Two

CHAPTER XI

CHIHUAHUA II

"I *banged* her, Coy," confessed Shane in desperation.

"Of course you, did, little brother, she is a fine piece of ass and what else is there to do in this miserable burg?"

I looked around the little breakfast nook to see whether she had come down from our room and was listenin' in, as she would be prone to do.

"I'd bang her myself if I got the chance," I whispered at him, "though *La Habanera* would cut off my dick. The State Bar has a rule, though; you can't bang a client, right? *That's* why you look so death-warmed-over upset. Right?"

"You don't understand. We have a *child.*"

"Not even you can work that quick. What the hell do you *mean*?" I demanded. "'Splain yourself, Lucy!"

I forked my *chilaquiles* carefully around my steaming plate as if they were chunks of lava in a molten sea. I began to arrange the soggy chips to depict 'The Play' at the end of the 'Big Game', Cal-Stanford football epic of 1980, and he explained, all right. He was practically in tears. The *coincidence* of all this was totally mind blowing. Of a one night stand becoming a major client, as if by sorcery. Shane seemed to be concerned with the ethics of not revealing to the Goldens that their little maid was once his *de facto* prime squeeze. And he was sure as hell concerned what would happen if his *wife*, that is Shane's wife, found out. She was not the type of girl we dated in college, you may be sure. She was a trophy wife, and like all trophy wives, concerned with *image*. So he was goddamned upset. I tried to calm him down.

"You are lucky that Belizeana (or her old man, they all have 'em) didn't come lookin' for you with a *shotgun*. She is the size of King Kong, for Chrissakes! *Way* too much woman for you, little brother." This didn't improve his mood.

"What the hell do you think I should do?" he asked.

"Follow the plan, man, follow the plan. You've come a long way since taking on the case. Too deep in to pull out. And she's out of trouble with the Feds, right? Let's keep on keepin' on. And say *nothing* of this to anyone, you goddamned idiot. And tell her to *forget* she's got a kid."

"She didn't tell the Goldens she had one."

"Of course she didn't. All she cares about is the job; all they care about is their son, right? Look. I want to cross examine Lili-o-Kulani here, your so-called paralegal, and make sure she's got down the correct moves, and a few other things. You go up and give comfort to – The Client. Ya get it? Go!"

Shane sent Alicia over to my table. She was dressed as she was before, like a Bluebird or whatever they have before Girl Scouts. 'Cept this time she was totin' a Bible. No Shit, Sherlock, she had a Bible gripped in one little brown hand.

"These puppies are *hot,*" I exclaimed, by way of diversion. And stopped eating the *chiaquiles*. "So you work for the great Shane as a paralegal," I began. "You don't look much like a paralegal."

"I have worked for Mr. Fitzgerald, Sir, for over six years. I help with the charity immigration work he does in Modesto." She had arrived in Chihuahua the previous evening by bus to assist Shane with translations, carrying a care package of props, I was told, prepared at Shane's direction, from Golden's wife.

"But you're not a *trained* paralegal, right, you never got a degree or anything like that?"

"*Sí.* I mean, *no.*"

"So you can't tell us whether a certificate of adoption issued in Chihuahua will be sufficient for a passport in the Department of Foreign Affairs in Mexico City?"

"Anything is sufficient if you give the *mordida* to the right official, Mr. Coy."

"And you have no trouble with that?"

"I do what Mr. Fitzgerald tells me to do. Anyway, Mr. Coy, your *novia* is the one with the connection in the *Departamiento de Justicia* here in Chihuahua, isn't it?"

"My girlfriend has a master's degree in treachery and deceit. That is why I was counting on *you* dotting the i's and crossing the t's – and watching *her.*"

"Ah, you might think it better to look toward your own canopy of stars."

You know, as I look back on it, *both* these women, Nelia and Alicia, spoke in abstract ways like vestal virgins, pretending to know a hell of a lot more about life than I did. Which I didn't find likely, by the way.

At this point, Shane and Nelia entered the little palm-thatched *bodega* where I was now wolfing down my breakfast. Habanera would meet us at 10:00 a.m. in, as she described it, 'our birth certificate store'.

"Good morning, Alicia," said Nelia in her ·thick Belizeana accent.

"Good morning, Madame," returned Alicia respectfully, and to Shane, "Good morning, Sir."

"That reminds me of a joke," Shane said, turning to me. "When I worked in the Philippines I had a secretary named Maternidad, who was a looker, I can tell you. So they must have named her Maternidad to warn men that if they dared navigate her curves she would morph into motherhood. In any event, one morning, Maternidad said: 'Sir, do you know the difference between a *good* secretary and a *grrreat* secretary? (and she rolled those r's in 'great' like a wave at Waikiki). And I said, 'No, Maternidad, but I am sure you are going to tell me.' And she replied, 'A *good* secretary says, 'Good morning, Sir' and a *grrreat* secretary says, 'Sir, its morning!'" He really told this joke. About 'navigating maternal curves', etc. This went over like a lead balloon. Not your 'A' game, little brother.

The appearance of Olelia rescued him. She did not disappoint, poured into pedal pushers that outlined the lips of her hungry vulva like a ripe star fruit. A gold lamé bra fought two papayas in harness, both trying to escape, their stems trained on some porno TV satellite above. A tattooed coral snake coiled around one ankle – the other sported a diamond tennis bracelet. A genuine ruby winked in the cute little *caldera* of her belly button. She must have had myriad weapons, spikes, scorpions, petards, chopsticks, perhaps even a tape recorder concealed in the tangled beaver dam of her hair, tinted silver and black, rising over her widow-peaked brow. I looked for the hilt of a stiletto in the elastic band of her thong but since she wore none it was probably hidden in her butt crack.

"You have the *dinero?*" she snarled, giving me a poke in the ribs with a Cruella de Ville index finger.

I handed over a large wad of greasy pesos, which she of course stuffed into the dark canyon of her crenellated cleavage.

"It will cost you more if I have to sleep with this guy," she warned.

"If you do, you'll kill him," says I, with dispassion.

Nelia and Alicia treated each other to a curdled Hollandaise look; they must have bonded as hotel roommates, for they were now a team.

In an ugly, squat, concrete cubicle on the town square, behind a particle-board desk, crouched a fat, pock-marked parricide. He was half-full of cheap mescal and a *gusano rojo* slept in the bottle's lees. A stack of papers and rubber stamp pad waited in the wings. Olelia was right: had this dude tried to play with her, he would have wound up on the desert sands like a clapped out *chili relleno*. Even she had her standards.

A black Trotsky vintage Underwood awaited his commands. A gang of mariachis and *abuelas* hung around waiting for something to go down. Histrionic bullshit flowed freely thereafter, including salutes to the Mexican flag, a serenade by the moribund musicians, oaths, mescal toasts, and *brazos* all around. A lot of money changed hands.

We left the building carrying an adoption certificate with more stamps and seals than a decree of Caesar Augustus.

"Where are we going from *here*?" asked *La Habanera* sweetly, in an attempt to keep the pesos flowing.

"*We* are not going anywhere but back," I told her firmly.

"*Aiyeeeeee*, you throw me away once again, after you get what you want. I will go with Shane to Mexico City . . . to keep him out of danger, of course." And she favored us all with a knowing smile.

"We will not put you to that trouble, *señora*," said Nelia, "we need to travel, as now gone Pancho Villa did, light in the saddle."

"I'm sure you'll be fine with your deewarf Bible thumper and the jolly black giant," grunted Olelia under her breath, grabbing me by the arm, and stalked off.

CHAPTER XII

IN THE ZONA ROSA

The Zona Rosa is named for the tony red light district it once used to be. It is an *inferior vena cava* of Mexico's *Distrito Federal*, the country's governmental and political heart. In the old days, red light designated the service providers; now the anonymous luminosity from countless computers illuminates the sex trade, which is strictly out call. *Zona Rosa* was the 'pink zone' long before gay folk became the dominant species. It finally grew into itself, one might say, after all.

For most of the day on May 30th, 1984, Manuel Buendía sat at his desk writing political columns for *El Día, El Sol de Mexico,* and his personal favorite, the so-called "Private Network." He copy edited the third draft of his fourth newspaper column revealing the links between the *Dirección Federal de Seguridad,* (DFS), the Mexican secret police, and Rafael Caro Quintero, the then reigning drug lord of Mexico. This particular article linked José Antonio Zorrilla, the Director of the DFS, with Quintero and his rival, Ernesto Fonseca.

The Zorrilla and Quintero mansions in Acapulco were but a block from each other; no one but Buendía thought this arrangement anything more than business as usual.

When he left his modest apartment in the suburbs as 6:00 a.m., Buendía's white *guayabera* was spotless; but it rained that morning and the short walk from his parking lot to the office left the garment spotted by raindrops infused by soot from the acid cloud trapped in the old volcanic caldera cradling the megalopolis. Used to this, he brought an extra garment for his speaking engagement at the International Association of Press Correspondents dinner in a hotel not far from the parking lot. His vestments must be as spotless as his journalistic reputation. He left his *Avenida Insurgentes* office at dusk, as the lights of the Zona Rosa twinkled to life. He was careful never to leave his car parked where he could not safely retrieve it after dark; he believed his enemies would not dare hit him in broad daylight: they might be seen. But, as we know, dusk is that magic time when shadows lengthen and the creatures of the night prepare nocturnal rituals.

As he inserted the key in the lock of the driver's side door of his Toyota Corolla, an assassin lodged five 38mm bullets in Buendía's back. The slugs from two exit wounds were never found; probably wound up in the lake bottom of Chapultapec Park.

Someone must be scapegoated, and quickly – that individuals, particularly tourists, can be arrested for crimes before they occur is unique to Mexican culture.

I do not panic easily. That noon, I dispatched Alicia and Nelia to the Department of Foreign Affairs with instructions to use the adoption certificate as the basis for a passport application. The office would open after *siesta* time at 2:00 p.m. Alicia was provided with a wad of 100 *peso* notes for any *mordida* that might become necessary, Nelia dressed to kill in one of the cast off second-wife costumes from *Nepotism,* pulled from the bag of tricks provided by Missy Golden. Linda Evans or some such had worn it to keep John Forsythe's eyes off Joan Collins. Nelia cloaked in gold lamé tinsel proved the wrong costume for a bureaucratic séance. I should have known that, right?

In any event, by dusk, by cocktail time, with my single margarita (Cointreau, Mexican lime juice, and Herradura *anejo* Tequila, over picked Truckee River ice, shaken – strike Truckee river ice. In the Ciudad de Mexico, substitute frozen cubes of Perrier), I began to worry. The Department of Foreign affairs was but two miles as the buzzard flies from the Hotel Crystal, where the girls had been parked in a suite two floors above mine. The Crystal was selected as a 5-star 'luxury' Mexican hotel; but like everything in downtown Mexico City, including the morning sky, it was more opaque than transparent, a Trebant cloaked in a Ferrari chassis. As armies of rats no doubt chase one another in concentric circles beneath the rococo stone facades of fountains, government buildings, and museums of Mexico City DF – the Crystal, like the night, concealed a thousand pair of eyes.

I hurried from the bar, to the elevator, to the lobby. My car and driver were at the curb; the girls must be in their suite getting ready for dinner or gossiping.

"*Donde estan las mujeres?*" I demanded of the driver. This terrified man, goggle-eyed and ready to bolt, responded, "*Corriendo, señor, hay las drogas*!" Say what? Drugs? This guy can't be serious. "*La policia – drogas – los mujeres incarcerado in el cuarto – usted, corriendo!*" The police had imprisoned the girls in their suite. I had best run like hell.

Thus was framed one of those half-dozen or so decisions, which re-direct or terminate a human life: the flight-or-fight syndrome.

Something had gone terribly wrong in the Department of Foreign Affairs, to be sure. Everyone knows that when foreigners are apprehended by Mexican police of any stripe, a sojourn in jail is mandatory. *Mordidas* paid by timid relatives at home, soon follow; these are initially characterized as liberating bribes, but once paid, morph into maintenance fees. Money is needed to keep the imprisoned in food, medical care, and so on – without which he or she might disappear forever. Once the mosquito tastes blood after the first skin prick, he is loath to discontinue sucking.

It is the same kind of revolving door racket as

California's[5] criminal justice system, but with extortive payments calibrated in non-honey coated cash: the Mexicans do not hypocritically characterize them as 'legal fees'. California's patchwork cloak of bail money, retainers for the attorneys, restitution payments, fines, *ad nauseam*, does no better a job of camouflaging corruption than the enveloping Mexican *serape* of *mordidas*.

In any event, I was at least bright enough to know that if a rescue were attempted, I would be swept into whatever net that had snagged my client and paralegal; and, once so imprisoned, communication with our support team in United States would be impossible. Mexican jail cells do not come equipped with telephones. I considered calling my office, Collie Green's office, and, yes, the office of Andrew Golden Productions, in order to warn them that we were about to be taken out of action. I owed the client a duty of prompt and accurate communication. Doing so now would signify failure, and would have immediately co-opted Golden in the web of *mordidas*. Who knew if telephone calls from the Crystal to the states were monitored? I would not take this risk, and selected the non-disclosure option.

After all, had I not successfully accomplished five of the seven steps necessary to satisfy the goals of the client? It is the sixth step of a staircase on which most people trip, on which those pushed from above crack their skulls. While options whirled like carousel horses in my conscious, my subconscious screamed – run like hell! Running would make me a double fugitive, would it not? A fugitive from the Mexicans' version of justice, and a fugitive from the client – for the immediate American construction of my failure to

---

[5] Much later, those creepy bastards Gray Davis and William Westwood 'Bill' Lockyer perfected this 'play for pay' syndrome right unto a 'fair-thee-well', almost bankrupting the state, guaranteeing the former a recall and the latter a meth-amphetamine addicted wife.

come to the client's aid would be: ABANDONMENT. And, the worst and most typical sin of all Americans' lawyers is client abandonment – which usually occurs the moment a client fails to pay that month's bill. But was the best way to aid Nelia seeking help from Big Brother to the North? Perhaps the lives of two women were at risk; and my dilly dallying could prove fatal.

"All right, assholes, let's rock and roll," I shouted at my subconscious, walking swiftly through the lobby toward the elevator doors, and whatever dark fate waited above.

CHAPTER XIII

IN THE ZONA ROSA II

The elevator doors at the eighth floor of Hotel Crystal, opening like stage curtains, framed a hotel security guard done up in a blue blazer, tie, and flannel trousers, shoulder to shoulder with a camo-garbed *federale*. They blocked the entrance to the double doors of Nelia and Alicia's suite. The goddamned hotel must be in on whatever scam was afoot!

I confronted the security guy and firmly, but in fractured Spanish, explained my rights as a guest, my role as a lawyer, demanded immediate access to the imprisoned Nelia and Alicia. The military dude in camo, as seen through the cellophane of a Toys R Us presentation box, wore a flat-topped cap, sunglasses, and trundled an automatic weapon in an aggressive way. A foot shorter than the security guard, he appeared at least twelve years of age. His juvenile mind labeled me a threat. Perhaps my fractured Spanish insulted his *duende*. He leapt forward and thrust the weapon against my chest. I saved myself from falling backwards by grabbing the barrel of the gun. The soldier reacted badly to this apparently hostile move, tried to twist the weapon from my hands. During the struggle for possession, its muzzle slammed into my right eye, shattered its hard contact lens, and drove the fragments into the iris.

Maddened by pain, and fully fed up with these taco peddlers, I pushed the soldier to the ground, and was about to brain him with the butt end of the rifle when the doors to the suite flew open. A giant Mexican in civilian clothes grabbed me by the shirt front with one hand, knocked the rifle from my hand to the floor with the other, and dragged me into the suite. He threw me on a couch, whipped a chrome-plated .38 upside my head and snarled, *"Tranquillo"* in a soft, simian, authoritative way. I noticed this guy wore a gold Rolex. It was not a fake – and a sure sign this guy was one of those who thought he might get out of this world alive. I went '*tranquillo,*' all right, prepared for my soul's imminent departure, when the young soldier, recovered and in possession of his rifle, tried to retrieve his honor by aiming at my head. 'José, Tranquillo' pulled his pistol away from my temple and trained it on the young soldier. In threatening *chilango* dialect he informed the kid that if he harmed this *gringo* he would send *him* to the next world (*proxima mundo*). Who *were* these evil circus wizards, and how did they relate to each other, if at all?

My damaged vision cleared sufficiently to scan the room. Alicia, forced to strip to bra and panties, sat on the edge of the bed, crying. I'd never lusted for her body parts *in flagrante* or otherwise, and found no delight in them now. Another thug pistol-whipped Nelia as she covered her head with her hands. They had not managed to get *her* to strip for them. The thug stopped what he was doing when I leapt from the couch and was immediately hammered back into place by a vicious blow from the giant thug. The suite had been dismantled: its lamps lay in pieces on the floor, faceplates had been removed from the electrical outlets, and stuffing from gutted mattresses flew about the room. Searching for *las drogas* no doubt. Why hadn't they just *planted* them in the girls' suitcases? Or maybe they had. I began to regret my putative bravery in attempting a rescue. The women didn't seem particularly glad to see me, either. Was I to blame as the true architect of their destruction?

I pulled another of my trump cards. Years ago I had been given a gold badge and a concealed weapons permit by the Contra Costa County's Sheriff's Office for saving a drowning child. They were contained in the kind of black leather wallet you see on TV. I pulled this from a back pocket and slapped it open on the glass table in front of the couch.

"Yo soy un investigador oficial de Los Estados Unidos," I snarled at the thug.

He stared at the badge for the briefest moment, then snarled back: *"Usted . . . usted es un federale FALSO!,"* grabbing my wrists, applying cuffs, throwing a blanket over Alicia as though she were a terrorist, then forcing us to shuffle out of the suite, into the hotel elevators, down onto the street, where a couple of vintage Chevrolet Camaros with chrome wheels and oversized tires waited to cart us away to God-knows-where.

A group of my fellow citizens, waiting to be herded to some event in their flowered shirts, looked on goggle eyed at what they naturally assumed to be a capture of drug trade mavens. It was no doubt the highlight of their South-of-the-Border Adventure.

CHAPTER XIV

IN THE LAIR OF
THE SECRET POLICE

Imagine a long unpaved dirt alley in the bowels of the capital city of Mexico. Imagine a series of GI sheeted hovels on either side, three-legged or half-dead mongrels foraging for whatever in the *basura*. The alley, dark as the interior of a swollen appendix, is lit only by the headlights of the souped-up Camaros the 'secret' police use as squad cars. The eyes of the dogs fire back reflections like agates in a child's game of chase. All well used dirt roads in Mexico have wash-boarded evenly spaced ruts, *topos*, as the Mexicans coyly call them. So the two-door Camaros and their passengers are shaken, not stirred, nigh unto death and the drivers curse softly under their breath. I am a passenger in one Camaro, the girls in another, thugs at the helm. 'José Tranquillo' is my driver and knows precisely where he is going. At first, I tried to memorize the road signs as we thundered along, but once out of the Zona Rosa, once out of the paved section of road in the capital city, once through the slums, there are no signs whatsoever. Like a gambler in a casino, a prisoner soon loses track of time and distance, and I am no exception. We are perhaps twelve miles or so from the Zona Rosa. I feel like mongrel droppings. How the hell did I manage to get myself and my clients caught up in a drug sting? It must have been that goddamned gold lamé dress. No, my guilt was more serious than that, more like ruptured hubris, the Oz-like planning of an over-achiever. The swan song of an ego, which preferred suicide to failure. The other lawyers turned down the case for a good reason: the seven strategies were stylish, perhaps even elegant, but not legally possible. Perhaps the Department of Foreign Affairs found it curious that a humble *campesina* in a housedress had adopted a 6'2" hooker. Perhaps Coy Coffin and his prime squeeze had fucked up the adoption papers. Perhaps I should have brought along Olelia, over the protests of my client. In any event, the thugs showed no lack of confidence in carrying forward their 'work'.

I realized that the Camaros are equipped with Motorola like radios; they slow down but do not stop. My driver barks an order into his microphone and the GI sheeted carapace of one hovel rolls back, revealing an opening lit sunrise bright. We roar into this space, the engines kill, and the GI sheeting swiftly descends. This is really one of the damnedest setups on the planet: the floor is polished concrete, the walls and roof are white porcelain tiles: at first you think you have landed in the intake lobby of Purgatory, but when you realize the thick glass windows on the right side of one wall are for viewing inmates, you suddenly imagine Hell might not be dark, but brightly lit to enhance suffering. Hidden behind this store front window is a catacomb of concrete cells, connected by very narrow passages. Each has its own corona of fluorescent lighting on twelve-foot ceilings.

We are photographed, processed, relieved of our belts, shoes, and socks. One of the thugs finds ten one hundred dollar bills I invariably keep in my left shoe; he sees that I see him grab them. We both know he is recorded by the security cameras, so, he jots something down on a bit of paper, faking it as a receipt. Of the various thugs on offer, this particular fellow displays a continuing look of pure malice, a look which says, 'I'm going to take great joy removing your *huevos.*' I glare back at him because money is power and he really doesn't know who the hell I am or of what I might be capable. I float into a Zen-like sort of trance that I maintain throughout my stay in this upside down tiled bathtub of a Gulag.

Each of us is given a separate adjoining cell in one of the catacombs farthest from the Purgatory lobby. The interior features of my cell taught me many things over the next several days. It had nothing inside except piles of crumpled newspaper and fast food cartons at one end, some cryptograms etched on a side wall, and a small (latched from the outside) window into which a jailer could view his captive. The cryptograms were in fact oblique hatch marks over vertical lines signifying the passage of time. One, two, three, four, five, six, hatch marks. Beneath one of these constructs, one prisoner had inscribed the Latin phrase attributable to Christ as he relinquished his soul on the cross. We were in a kind of death row. I did not interpret this as a good sign. My calculations revealed that the cell's previous occupant languished thirty-seven days before he was shot/hanged/garroted or fed to the dogs. I listened for the oink oink oink of large swine, because that is one of the ways Mexicans, particularly those linked to the drug trade, dispose of corpses. Since there was no light in the cell other than invasive fluorescence, it was difficult to work out the time; but if my predecessors had been able to mark the passage of days with hieroglyphs, why could I not follow suit? I thought I heard roosters (one hears them every morning in Mexico; they are as much a part of the culture of time as the chiming of church bells.) But I heard no hogs.

Hours or a day later, the cell door opened and I was handed a Melmac plate with a tortilla welded to a refried bean cow patty. And a plastic glass of water topped with dead gnats. 'Fuck this shit,' I said to myself, and handed the tray back to one of my captors, who seemed most offended that I should reject his offering.

I worked out that the tortilla-cum-shit arrived at about 6:00 a.m. soon after the rooster crowed.

I wished for a tallow candle, so I could charcoal the walls with images of minotaurs, anubii, Volkswagen beetles, fossilized tortillas, or a procession of gnome-like creatures with bad-ass looks bringing me fossilized tortillas stuck together with dog spew, and I of course would be the shaman in a kind of a feathered headdress. I had neither stylus nor brush, not even a pencil stub, but I found a loose screw in a small air vent, which had been dislodged and replaced many times before, kind of a legacy from those who had bought the farm before me, after trying to escape. And it must have been the instrument for creating the wall calendars.

It didn't take long for the evil-countenanced captor to open my cell, again, offering me a receipt to sign – a receipt for seven hundred dollars. I reasoned that once he had my signature on this document, I was of no further use to him so I told him, politely, to fuck off, fuck his mother, or have his mother fucked by a succession of iguanas (since he was certainly of reptilian patrimony). He didn't take this well either.

The next evening, God knows when it was, I began to sift through the newspapers at the back of my cell. I found two things of interest: the first was a desiccated Kentucky Fried Chicken box (and some bones – now I might be able get a good Cro-Magnon cave-fire going and air brush the carbon on the walls by blowing through the chicken bone!), and the second was a card, four and a half inches by six, that was printed in brightly colored blue ink – the kind of card that used to come in newspapers for ordering cassette tapes. It was in Spanish, but embossed in such a way that if you scratched its surface, a white line would emerge from behind the blue ink. The KFC box, on the other hand, was so brittle it could be fashioned into a hand tool. It took me a couple of days, or what I measured as days, to work out that fact that it might be inserted between the little door in the cell and its frame, to lift the latch that secured the porthole.

Now, this was the era of the first Reagan administration, and his posse numbered a few characters. An actor, John Gavin, served as Ambassador to Mexico. One of the cabinet members was an old lawyer friend, one who had as much training and experience for his position as had Gavin in statesmanship. But, he was a fun guy who flew around in his own Department of the Navy DC-9 and, by chance, while dating his secretary as a way of keeping close to him, I memorized his inside telephone number. So with the screw, I scratched his name and number on the blue cassette card and shoved it in my butt crack, for future use. With the KFC box chisel/dagger/putty-knife/screwdriver, I lifted the metal latch and pushed open the porthole. When I thought the coast was clear, I stuck my nose into the corridor in front of our cells.

Two security cameras at either end scanned the narrow hallway. But, since this was a Mexican hoosegow, they were not in sync! So when both swung in an arc away from my cell, I could, for several seconds, poke my nose through the porthole and look about. There was not a great deal of lateral range, but I could see down to where, believe it or not, a combination Master padlock secured my cell. I took a long hard look at this puppy and with an extension of my KFC box tool was able to move it aside so as to read the model number on its back. It would be unlikely that I could ever get the code, and, even so, I would never be able to reach the padlock to open it.

I finally determined that Nelia was housed in the cell to the left of me, Alicia to the left of her. I did not discover this by shouting through the window, but by tapping out Morse code on the wall. Where Nelia had learned Morse was a mystery, but she responded accurately and was able to report on the threats made against her and Alicia. God bless the Boy Scouts of America!

The thugs had given them confessions to sign implicating me as the head of a Honduran drug cartel for which they were the mules! The confessions contained an admission of the murder of a Mexican journalist. These revelations came after hours of tap tap tapping, and I finally fell, exhausted, into my first deep sleep after having been put in this hellhole.

It seemed to me eons passed; I was no longer offered water and food; the girls were apparently holding up and Nelia's tapping revealed they had consumed six meals and been escorted to the *bano* as many times. I had indeed heard their cell doors slam, and hoped they might not be cooperating with the thugs.

On perhaps the fifth day, I felt kind of logy. Dehydration was beginning to work on my imagination. I had a dream where Nelia was fucking me in the cell while Alicia took notes for the afterlife in her little Bible book, clucking away like a disapproving old hen.

I had another dream where I was at the 21 club with Andrew Golden discussing the status of Nelia's case; he ordered rare hamburgers as thick as a Sumo wrestler's fist, garnished with Bermuda onions, ripe tomatoes, washed down by old burgundy and ice water in Lalique pitchers. For some reason we then went to see the Rockettes.

What woke me was not a hankering for club soda and lime, but another thug with a *second* Melmac plate of beans and tortilla, another cup of water. Though thirsty, I maintained the correct macho modality and knocked the mug out of the guy's hand. He tried to catch mine while slamming the cell door, but was I able to remove it just in time.

On the evening of that day, as I best recollect, for I was losing short term memory, a slick thug with very good English entered the cell and presented me with Spanish legal documents complete with English translation which, indeed, characterized my tenure in Mexico as the chief of a drug gang which employed Nelia and Alicia as mules, and that Nelia's visit to the Department of Foreign Affairs was prompted by the necessity for a passport in aid of drug smuggling. Thrown in for good measure, gratuitously, was a charge of homicide for offing one Manuel Buendía, in the Zona Rosa, on May

30th, 1984, the apparent motive for which was to silence an article he had in process characterizing us as drug warlord and serfs.

At this point, I did not refuse to sign the document. I knew that, by international treaty and convention, nationals imprisoned in foreign countries are entitled to ask their captors to inform their consul of incarceration, and demand an interview. So I told the thug that after I had had the benefit of a conference with a United States consul, I would consider signing the document. He informed that this would be impossible, that in order to see the consul I would first have to sign the document. I told him, in English, to fuck off and leave me alone. He then claimed Alicia and Nelia had already executed their copies of the documents. I told him, "So what?"

He made various threats of this, that, and the other, including one to deprive me of food and water. I told him, in essence, "Hell, that's a benefit, that's why I'm still here for you to harass."

Just to emphasize my contempt, I peed in a corner of the cell while he was in there brandishing the paperwork. He stayed inside the cell a long time until again I pulled down my pants, at which time he waltzed out.

It must have been the next morning that the 'good-cop' in the cast opened my cell, roughly cuffed me, and marched me through the hall, in a line with my cellmates. First was Alicia, who still madly clutched her Bible, then Nelia, then myself. A longhaired young girl of sixteen, at most eighteen, wearing Indian garb, followed behind.

We were brought into that holding area which had those windows overlooking the inverted tile bathtub lobby. Several individuals took inventory of our group, but the one who gave me the most hope was a chubby young American who, I assumed, was from the American consular office. I demanded of our captor to speak with him, and was summarily ignored. The young man viewed me with interest. I found out later it was his job to troll Mexican prisons for Americans lawfully charged with crime, and those who were wrongfully imprisoned by way of extortion. I repeated loudly, in English, so he could see me and my demands to speak with him. The thugs pushed me away from the window and told me in Spanish to shut up.

I turned away from the glass as though to moon my captors, reached in my butt crack as though giving it a scratch, and dislodged the blue card so it fell down my pant leg and onto the floor. The American guy did not react to this and I hoped like hell the stupid Mexicans had missed it. I caught his eye and I pointed to the floor. He briefly put his finger to his lips and began to speak with one of the Mexican thugs, so as to distract him. I did not know how he could retrieve the card, or whether he would try. But our presence in this hellhole was now known to outsiders, and relief might be possible. I gave Nelia and Alicia high signs, and I received in return wan smiles of encouragement.

CHAPTER XV

IN THE PALACE OF THE WINDSORS

Ronald Wilson Reagan never retired for the evening without a feeling of wonder that an amateur sportscaster from Illinois had wound up President of the United States. The position never changed his sense of personal power – no more than watching reruns of himself as the emcee of *Twenty Mule Team Borax*. John Lennon described, in one of his songs, the President's state of mind, when he woke in a huge featherbed on that June morning:

> *And though she feels as if she's in a play*
> *She is, anyway*

President Reagan never had a clue as to John Lennon's state of mind. He tried to capture, in his journal entry for that day, the sense of unreality he felt while trying to find his bed in the vast Marlborough suite of Buckingham Palace after a gala state dinner. Sentinels representing life-sized portraits of old uniformed generals, nobles, courtesans, great ladies, whomever, stared at him expectantly. He wondered if his biographical notes should be written objectively, from the standpoint of how others were thought to perceive him, or, subjectively, with continuing obeisance to his higher power, which governed his relatively simple and straightforward nature. He sighed, donned a pair of silk pajamas with the seal of the President of the United States on the pocket, covering the scar from an assassin's bullet, and crawled into another large featherbed beside a sleeping Nancy. They had been given identical king-sized beds in the suite. His wife slept soundly, probably suffering from jet lag. He nodded off in a moment.

When he awoke, a daily agenda placed on his bedside table the night before reminded him of a scheduled breakfast with the Queen and her Duke of Earl, Reagan's secret name for Edinburgh. Omelets filled with Chasen's chili, flown over on Air Force 1, were on offer. 'Cabbage', the Duke of Earl's nickname for his wife, carefully concealed her passion for Mexican food. No hot-sauce was to be found on QEII's upper lip. The Reagans and the Windsors genuinely enjoyed one another's company, joking that their sons Charles and Ron Jr. were so much alike, it was certain neither of them would end up as either King of England or President of the United States. The Duke marveled at Reagan's sunny disposition, but let Cabbage deal with Nancy; he, too, had become addicted to chili omelets and bounded in dressed like Grendel, from either his hounds or hookers. The Duke reminded Reagan of the constipated baboon with whom he co-starred in a barely remembered grade B movie.

All were now seated in a garden anteroom adjoining the suite, about to dig into chili omelets topped with Wisconsin cheddar cheese, Petaluma sour cream, and Vidalia onions served on Wedgewood, when aide Michael Deaver arrived at table with a secured radio-phone.

"It's Andrew Golden, the producer, calling from the States, Sir, urgent, cleared through the White House." Reagan treated the table to one of his buoyant head-cocked Gipper grins and cupped the receiver with his hand.

"Here's our friend who owns the beach house we were telling you about last evening: he's the *Nepotism* guy who can give Lady Katherine, right (?), an audition. Excuse me, this can't take long."

"We are absolutely over the top," whispered the Queen, "about *Nepotism*; fiercely addicted to it. We are having Mr. Golden over to luncheon later this month."

"Well, perhaps that's why he's calling! Andy . . . it must

be midnight in Los Angeles. I'm having breakfast. What's up?"

"Mr. President, please forgive this intrusion. But the matter is urgent, at least it is to us, and involves little Sandy."

"Well, what's urgent to you is also to me. What's up?"

"You know our boy is – physically challenged – so we hired this Nanny to take care of him and he became overly attached. We later discovered she is illegal."

"We all have *those* servant problems, Andy, the damned INS."

"So when we asked her for her papers she bolted and Sandy went into shock."

"For heaven's sake."

"We hired this lawyer to find her and fix her paperwork, but he has managed to get himself, his legal assistant, and our Nelia . . ."

"You mean that tall black gal who looks like Carmen Miranda without the fruit hat?"

"The same. He managed to get them charged with the murder of a Mexican journalist and they are being held by the Mexican Secret Police."

"Whoa hoss, whoa. You don't mean to say that the lawyer *murdered* a Mexican national *in* Mexico, do you?"

"No, no, none of them could write *that* script. My people think it's the usual Mexican shake down; what can happen to American tourists down there."

"So what can I do to help?"

"Can you direct the Embassy in Mexico City to intervene and obtain their release?"

"Well. Jack Gavin (you remember him, he used to be an

actor), is our man down there. I'll ask him to have them cut loose without starting a war. And Andy. You will owe us a week at the beach house and a job for my pretty breakfast companion's niece," (winking at the Queen.)

"Now Ronnie," said the First Lady, "tell Andy you're having breakfast. You can always talk to him later. This is not Malibu."

"Got to run," said Reagan, "boss is calling. I'll report back."

"Thank you Ronnie," said Andrew Golden.

He handed the phone back to Deaver. Sopped up some chili with a chunk of San Francisco sourdough bread, none the worse for wear after its flight over the Atlantic, popped it in his mouth, and furrowed his brow.

"Mike, after breakfast, and before this morning's security briefing, get me Jack Gavin on the phone in Mexico City. Wake him up, if necessary."

CHAPTER XVI

IN THE MIND OF NELIA

Dios mío? Who *is* this man who keeps coming back to me?

First, he plants a bun in my oven on Caya Esmeralda – now, this. Of course, he is not to blame; I wouldn't let him wear one of those Greek raincoats or whatever. My pride, my religion. I wanted to addict him to my velvet skin.

Then, because of Esmé I am forced to go north. Why did I end up doing so? Because I didn't tell him about her. I had no way to find him. He would have paid. Why hide her? Because any woman of salt in San Ignacio would behave the same; Belizeanas are not beggars. I also must take blame she is defective – that is the truth of it, no?

And now. *He* tries to rescue *me*. A second time. Consciously, or not. Who knows? Because I have been forced to flee, up, down, and now back again – like some *pelota* flying across this false rainbow of a border.

He has tried to rescue me *three times* – each resulting in strange, unhappy endings. Of course, Esmé is not an unhappy ending. It is almost as though his actions are intended to spawn chapters in a novel he wants to write. Some would-be writers are like that.

It explains why he uses defective creatures as tools, that cactus-coma Coy boy bloke and his *puta, La Habanera* – so intentionally *reckless*. They are like those stooges, no?

On the other hand, the latest rescue was most brave. He knew he would sustain great loss, just as he managed on Caya Esmeralda. But his gallantry lands me in a place where I am certain to die, absent some miracle.

Oh, for just five minutes with my ab iron. I would smash in the brains of these *spic sapos*. Dare threaten my child! Threaten *our* child! Threaten the offspring of La Avitia, who wouldn't let this scum kiss her feet. When I tell my man they have done this, he will kill them somehow, some way, some day. Just in exchange for the threat. Even though I told him he is weak. I just wanted to hurt him, just a little. He is so smug.

The one I worry for is the poor paralegal. She is out of her mind with fright, and doesn't know what she should do. She never imagined herself in this kind of trouble. She is a good one, though.

Life is a series of contradictions, isn't it so? Puzzle fragments dumped from a stardust box into each naked lap. We each get the same number of pieces. It is our fate to make them fit. There is no 'good' or 'bad' little dimple or bump, just a slew of potential connections. Many mistakes must transpire before one can even begin to define an accurate picture. To try to force them together, to go against the flow, only promotes inception of disease, invites early death. I wonder if I will have the chance to teach Esmé that, and that there is no 'bad' grain of stardust. That's why it took some bloke who can't move or speak to discover the engine that redistributes the stuff throughout the cosmos.

Making the sign of the cross is only a justification for these *sapos* to release their venom.

Alicia had better watch herself.

CHAPTER XVII

IN THE LAIR OF
THE SECRET POLICE II

Before being led back to our individual cells, during the viewing, we had a chance to whisper to one another. I learned more about the various additional documents forced upon the girls, including more confessions relative to drug dealing, admissions to conspiracies to murder Mexican journalists, and so on. They had refused to sign anything and been slapped around in return. They had eaten the rubbish served them and made numerous trips to the loo.

I also got a good look at the young Indian girl, with gorgeous plaited shining hair and a fierce determined look, whose stubborn gaze focused on the floor.

On one occasion when Nelia refused to sign, the evil-faced jailor presented her with a picture of Esmé, retrieved from her wallet, with the logo of a photographer in Belize. San Ignacio was close to the Mexican border, and they threatened, if she refused to sign, to send confederates of the secret police to kidnap the child, hold her hostage until she did. Nelia was beside herself about this threat but smart enough not to panic. What I understood, but she had no time to say, was that the confessions implicated me as ringleader, but I knew she would not do anything to compound the trouble conjured by my reckless lawyering. She asked if she should sign and I told her to wait, though I could not link any timing to the surreptitious dropping of the note, which I could only hope would bear fruit.

After the consular visit, the tension in the jail suddenly mounted. I was again presented the confession for signature. I again declined, using the excuse there had been no chance to speak with the consular officer. This time, there were two thugs on hand; one slapped me so hard I fell against the rear concrete wall of the cell. I wanted to kill this guy, shouted as many stinging insults as I could re-create from my limited Spanish vocabulary to further my macho fiction; the thugs promised something '*muy malo*' would happen to 'my mules', as they called Alicia and Nelia, that very evening.

Indeed.

I don't know how many hours later the beatings began. But echoes of the pistols, bludgeons, and truncheons striking human flesh, the piteous cries accompanying the blows, came from the cell to my right. They ceased as suddenly as they began. My Kentucky Fried Chicken tool pried open the latch so I could peer into the corridor. My captors tossed the now naked Indian woman from her cell. One thug, holding each of her feet, dragged her slowly by my cell so that her beautiful corona of hair, now un-plaited, painted the corridor floor with her freshly spilled blood.

My conscience rained upon me blows of responsibility for this death. Volcanic rage of retaliation fought with guilt. These cowards. The girl could have been no more than eighteen; what had she done to deserve such a fate?

I wondered if I should sign the damn documents. What if the next to go were Nelia, or Alicia? The clear implication was that either could be next.

CHAPTER XVIII

IN THE MIND OF ALICIA

I will be the next to be murdered. And I deserve it. Thank God, I am not good looking or I would be raped in addition. And I can see them looking at my gold fillings, the ones bought with a bonus Boss gave me to fix my rotten teeth. They will take them out with screwdrivers. The Christian martyrs got extra credit toward sainthood for being raped; I don't think being raped is going to earn me any extra credit. I don't mean to say that, dear God, but I have forgotten the priest term for it. Dispensations, that is what it is. I don't think being raped will gain me any dispensations. And I don't want to go to heaven, hell, or purgatory with holes in my teeth – like a dead sea urchin.

So I am hoping they will just kill me instead of raping me first but that will be up to them. I am going to keep my mouth shut the whole time and they are not going to be able to do anything with it. I am not going to remind them of my fillings. Though I think my curly hair is good looking, I have never read a magazine about a raped girl who had curls like mine. The Boss was counting on me to make sure the adoption certificate would work; and I am not sure if it is my mistake interpreting Mexican law, or whether that *puta Habanera* sold us out, like Judas, for a handful of silver. But maybe this thing has to do with something beyond us all, because some of the paperwork they now want me to sign makes me a murderer. And I will never admit to that, not only because I murdered no one, but because lying about committing a mortal sin can be as bad as the mortal sin itself. I don't want to get myself caught in that trap. None of us committed a murder trying to help Nelia. God forgive me, but I have never even had a speeding ticket.

When I study the marks on my wall, it makes me cry.

They are the last scratchings of dead people. But I cannot remove them from my mind, and they march in front of my eyes when I try to sleep, which I have not done since I have been here. The marks mean that the prisoners before me never came back. It is lucky I have neither child nor husband. Well, I have a husband, but he is a drunk and wouldn't miss my going. So there will be few people to mourn; not even my Boss because he will be dead soon after me. The Indian woman is now gone and I am next.

What was *her* sin? I could not catch her eye when we were in the room of tiles. What could she have done that was wrong? Maybe she was a *revolucionaria*.

I don't have much on my conscience. I lusted after some men but got nowhere with them, so what is the sin in that? And my lust wasn't much compared with lust I have read about. I do not believe one can commit a sin in one's mind unless it is acted upon. I have done my devotionals, my Stations of the Cross, I have taken Christ into my heart. I have paid my dues, as the *gringos* like to say.

Why kill my Boss? The only reason I am here is because I work with the poor *campesinos* in the Central Valley he tries to help. He fights as hard for them as he does for the people who pay. He asked me to come along as a translator because, well, sometimes his Spanish is ridiculous. He always says he is '*embarazada*' instead of 'sorry' – but he could never be pregnant that often, and anyway, he is a man. He always says I am a kind of saint but *he* is the real one, because I get paid and usually he never does, at least, never by the poor. I have even seen him turn down beautiful girls offered by their fathers for green cards, right before their *quinceañera*. They are promised him for a night in exchange for bond money, for legal fees, for their families being placed at the beginning of the immigration line. He probably understands it would really be an honor for a girl to be with my Boss, and the family's hope is that there might be a

United States *niño* or *niña* in the offing. I pray I never have to explain what happened, this time, to Mrs. Boss. She has not liked me since I kidnapped the little heathen daughter and brought her to church one Sunday when I was babysitting for the weekend.

That one is a kind of *brujita*, and told her mother on me immediately; I almost lost my job with the Boss. And it is not true, dear God, that I then waxed that woman's kitchen floor, so that she would slip and fall and break her hip. I did not link waxing the floor to any kind of revenge, to bad feelings on my part. Again, the Boss intervened and kept me from being fired.

Those children will be broken if my Boss is murdered. I think that will be the way of things here; and, if I don't sign these official papers, will they kill me next? Then Nelia? Then they will kill Boss. If they kill Nelia, they might as well kill Boss, because he could never accept that. He could never live it down. It would be for him the ultimate failure. They may tell Nelia she must sign the papers to try to save him; she has a strange look about her that is very much like the look of love. She could break my back with one blow from her hand. She is a giantess out of a fairy tale book, and very brave. When they were trying to get her to strip in the hotel room I never imagined a woman could know so many bad words or *spit them out* like machine-gun fire. She scared them. She has eyes like a panther. *Those* scared them. They scare *me*. She looks like she could tear you apart.

I stripped right away and they could do anything they wanted, but of course, they didn't want to do anything. I am not the kind of woman that would ever have to be worried about being raped.

CHAPTER XIX

IN THE WEST WING

It was the choke in Joan Simpson's voice on the intercom as she alerted him to an incoming call from the Embassy in Mexico City that intrigued Secretary of the Interior John 'the Mongoose' Hartington.

He reclined his leather swivel chair nigh unto the breaking point, studying a plan to store surplus oil: Utah's natural salt domes as a counter measure against OPEC price fluctuations. He must have put on forty pounds since coming to Washington with Ronald Reagan. He would have to enroll in Pritikin in Santa Monica. The elevational drawings for the subsurface salt dome storage facility rested on the easel of his expanding gut; the President was forced to attend the same banquets, eat the same rich food, yet *he* didn't seem to gain an ounce. He would have to get one of those 'wheels', a device Reagan brought with him wherever he traveled, a device which could even be used in Air Force One to coil and uncoil like an inchworm in the center aisle of the aircraft. It took care of the stomach muscles, torso, and arms. Actors had all sorts of tricks to homogenize their image. Hartington would just have to stop eating canapés and drinking double martinis; but they were necessary to abate the stink of Washington D.C.'s bureaucratic sewer. 'The Mongoose' was the President's chief rat exterminator, and he relished the job. He imagined Joan's 38D rack resting on her desktop as her diaphragm heaved against the tension apparently caused by this incoming call.

Hartington enjoyed observing waiting bureaucrats focus on Joan's breasts by means of a small monitor in one of the drawers of his large antique desk. He found it useful to get right to the core of a person's weaknesses and strengths. He gave nothing away with the décor of his office; his Stanford undergraduate degree, his admissions to the California Supreme Court, a picture of his family, and a photo of him and the President riding horses at the *Rancheros Vistadores* pageant in Santa Barbara. Those simple adornments told visiting guests everything he needed them to know about him and nothing more.

"Mr. Secretary," she breathed, "you know your friend Shane Fitzgerald?"

"I thought he was *your* friend now, Joan," joked Hartington, "what about him?"

"A consular officer from the Embassy in Mexico City is on your private line wanting to speak to you – apparently Shane is in a Mexican jail charged with murder."

"That wild man," muttered Hartington, "put the guy on."

"Mr. Secretary, my name is Buck Gogarty."

"You are making that name up, of course? Who the hell are you, really? You have some Irish connection. But you're calling from Mexico . . ."

"That's correct, sir. Excuse me for using your private White House line. But I got the number in a strange way. I am a consular officer in our Embassy in Mexico City and part of my assignment is jail visitation to determine if any American citizens have been imprisoned, rightly or wrongly, and offer them aid. And we happened to visit the holding facility of the Mexican Secret Police, where they house truly dangerous criminals, and Shane Fitzgerald, whom I now understand to be a California attorney, dropped a scrap of paper with your phone number and name scratched on it. I was able to retrieve it by bribing one of the jailers."

"What did that crazy idiot Shane *do,* Consul Gogarty? Get in a fight with some hooker, hit some *federale* over the head with a bottle of Pacifico?" He typed his caller's name in the so-called 'Kitchen Cabinet' database to determine whether he was political or career State department.

"No, sir, nothing as simple as that. He is charged with the premeditated assassination of Manuel Buendía, a muck-raking journalist, but a famous and highly respected one, in the Zona Rosa. And there are two women imprisoned with him, I found out, apparently his secretary, one Alicia Rojas, and the other, a woman known only as Nelia, both charged as co-conspirators. And there are allegations of drug dealing as the motive. Apparently Buendía was about to publish an article exposing Fitzgerald."

"Holy shit, son," exclaimed Hartington, bouncing upright in his chair, "you must be kidding. Shane is no murderer – worked for the President during the campaign. He has four kids and is *death* on drugs. I happen to know this: we come from the same town, were office mates, belong to the same club. Shane is a bit of a cowboy, but a good guy. Consul Gogarty – you do everything you can to protect all three of these American citizens, starting now."

Harrington considered his last comment – giving an order to a Consular Officer – as beyond his authority. He should go through George Shultz, Secretary of State, directly; or the Undersecretary for Latin American affairs, whose name he could not recall; or at a minimum, contact the Mexican desk at State.

Then he remembered: while acting as Appointments Secretary of President Reagan, he interviewed and approved the appointment of Jack Gavin as Ambassador to Mexico. George Shultz was traveling with the President in London attending a formal state dinner. Six o'clock in D.C., midnight in London. Mexico City was on Mountain Time, or was it central time? So the Embassy was probably closed, and this young man was working after hours.

"Strike what I just said, Consul. On behalf of Shane and his family, and on behalf of our country, I thank you for your service. Just hang tight, make sure nothing awful befalls them, and you will be hearing through the appropriate channels what move you should make."

"Thank you sir, I shall stand by." And Hartington hung up the phone, gravely worried for his friend.

He assumed that by now Joan was sobbing. Shane had this miraculous way of entraining the opposite sex; 'The Mongoose' had experienced this too many times on the campaign trail while trying to reach that boy for an early morning briefing. He typed in Jack Gavin's name in the 'Kitchen Cabinet' directory and found a line into the Ambassador's residence in Mexico City.

He buzzed Joan.

"Not to worry, dear, help is on the way. Dial this number for me in Mexico and get Ambassador Gavin on the phone."

"Thank God," said Joan softly.

"Don't be thanking anyone; these things are not over until they're over."

Joan reported that Ambassador Gavin was in Zacatecas giving a speech to the Mexican Chamber of commerce.

"I don't give a shit if he's in Cucamonga. Tell whoever is fielding his calls that this is an emergency and have him get back to me *like now.*"

CHAPTER XX

IN THE MINISTRY OF JUSTICE

I had always wanted to ride in the back of a Brinks truck. And on this smoggy dusky Mexican morning, I got my chance. They backed it up to the *cloaca maxima* of the camouflaged prison and loaded us inside. The truck had juxtaposed benches like one of Golden's limousines, except along its sides, and less plush. Waiting inside was an articulate Mexican who spoke better English than I, identified himself as a graduate of Harvard Law School and clearly not a thug. His card identified him as an associate with the Ministry of Justice. He didn't speak of drugs, of Manuel Buendía, of murder charges, of neither cabbages nor kings, but about the various violations of Mexican law perpetrated by what he described as my 'reckless lawyering'.

It is embarrassing to be taken down in front of a client and your own employee, by a guy this well prepared.

"So, we start with the fraudulent adoption certificate. Don't you think that rang some bells in our Ministry of Foreign Affairs?"

"What does it have to do with murdering a Mexican journalist?"

"It has to do with a California lawyer perpetrating a fraud on a Mexican tribunal. And we found this paperwork in your briefcase – the excuse for obtaining a United States visa was that Ms. Nelia was going to become a contestant *on some game show*? What about this letter stating that she must be examined at Stanford University to determine if she has a rare skin cancer?"

He was referring to my 'bag of tricks', a letter that the Goldens had conjured up inviting Nelia to be a contestant on *The Dating Game,* and a 'medical necessity' letter, all lying in wait to justify issuance of a tourist visa.

"What about them? Those have not been presented to anyone. *Damnum absque injuria,* Counsel!" (I could throw Latin around with the best of them and Sturdy Golden Bears trumped Harvard nerds, even at 6:00 a.m.)

"And, in any event," I continued, "what does attorney work product privileged documents have to do with your boys murdering an innocent girl to get me to sign a trumped up confession? My client certainly should be examined at Stanford after her treatment by your goons in that cute little *Gulag,* doncha think?"

I was not going to admit anything to this bright young man.

"Don't worry, Mr. Fitzgerald, you probably all will be released without charges. We just wanted to let you know that we had probable cause for arresting and confining you."

I decided to let that one go. As my mentor said, "You can slide further on shit than you can on sand."

"Your command of the English language is excellent," I said.

"We have nothing to do with those people in the jail, you understand. We are with the Ministry of Justice," he said, by way of distancing himself from the events in the jail. But I couldn't help but get in another dig.

"Yes. Those pigs in the jail are with the Ministry of *Injustice,* Murder Incorporated. You are with just a *different* branch of the Mexican government."

He gave me a wan, bitter smile.

The Brinks truck came to rest in a square of the type you

might see in Madrid or Barcelona, surrounded by stone colonnades. There was too much murk and mire in the sky to determine the position of the sun; everything was bathed in dark greenish shadows. We were led into a large ante chamber and greeted by a man in a suit, wearing yet another gold Rolex, who had the demeanor of someone just rousted out of bed with his mistress. You could spend days in the United States Department of Justice and never find anyone wearing a Swiss watch.

This guy walked up to me and identified himself, in English as the Mexican Minister of Justice. I don't remember his name. He leaned forward and softly said: "You are very lucky you have such powerful friends."

"Yes," I told him, thinking he meant John Hartington, "They are most powerful indeed."

I pointed to his watch. "When are you going to let us go?"

"Patience, Mr. Fitzgerald, paperwork must be prepared to satisfy everyone's interests. This will take six hours. You have ruffled significant feathers in this town. And, as I am sure you have been advised, your conduct, as they say, is not beyond reproach."

I decided not to argue the point.

"Is there anything I can get you while you are waiting?" he asked, not discourteously.

"Yes. I could use a telephone."

"You are welcome to use the one in my office."

"And I don't want the line tapped or the conversation recorded, OK?"

"You do Mexico (he pronounced it 'Mehico') an injustice, Mr. Fitzgerald. You are no longer at that level."

"Forgive me."

He opened the door to his ornate office, decorated with Aztec pottery, and instructed me in the use of his telephone. My first duty was to call Andrew Golden, who was apparently waiting for my call. After asking about Nelia and my well-being, he said, "Damn, Shane, you are a stud. I would have run like hell."

"At the time, part of me wanted do exactly that."

"Well, your loyalty will be rewarded. Stay on point. The President just phoned from London and tells me you will be released in the next six hours."

"The President of *what*?"

"The President, Shane, of the United States of America. Stay calm. Stay on point. Try to get the job done but get it done without any further jeopardy to anyone's life, including your own, if you take my meaning."

"Yes sir. I shall give it my best shot. Call my family, please and let them know we are OK." And I gave him the number.

I asked the Minister of Justice if it would indeed take another six hours for us to be released. He augured, now, a shorter time than that. Marine Guards were en route from the Embassy to escort the Brinks van to some hotel in downtown Mexico.

Marine Guards, lions, tigers and bears, oh my. We had really opened a can of worms, and I couldn't imagine it closing without several of my fingers chopped off in retribution. There is a price for hubris, roughly in proportion to its degree. Think of Achilles' heel.

Two marines, in full embassy dress, red white and blue with gold braids, brandishing weapons, roared up in a jeep. We were bundled back into the Brinks truck and the entourage swept off into the Mexican dawn.

CHAPTER XXI

IN THE ZONA ROSA III

We found ourselves once again in the Zona Rosa, checked this time into the Maria Isabel Sheraton and escorted to a suite with adjoining bedrooms on the 14th floor. At least this place had an American brand. The Marines treated us as they might foreign dignitaries: "Ambassador Gavin welcomes you to Mexico, Sir. We shall be at either end of the hall providing security. Should you need anything, just signal us on this intercom." One handed me a Motorola handset, saluted sharply, and left to take his post.

Our suitcases had been repacked, recovered, and brought into the suite by a bellman. They did not contain my thousand dollars. No big deal at this point, right?

Each of us spent delicious hours in the bathroom, removing the grit and the stench of the prison. I had a long séance with the lavatory, realizing that I had neither food nor drink for at least five days, and no bodily functions to speak of other than urination, which became less frequent during the captivity. We were all bone tired. After donning bathrobes, we huddled together in a circle holding hands on the huge bed that dominated the master bedroom of the suite, giving thanks for our liberation. Those who say tragedies come in threes may be right: at this moment of thanksgiving, the room began to shake. A 5.6 magnitude earthquake was having its way with the human works of improvement in the *caldera*. "What can happen next?" I marveled. We soon wrapped ourselves in various parts of the covers like *enchiladas suizas* and fell into deep sleep.

Sometime thereafter, I was awakened by a ringing telephone. It was 'Collie' Green.

"Shane. Collie here. Understand you have had a few

problems. Listen. You are on the five-yard line with five minutes to go in the second half. Just put your head down and *run* that ball over the goal line."

"A *few* problems???? I'd like to *kick you* across the goal line, Collie," I said, greatly annoyed and half-asleep.

"I didn't get you arrested for murder, old son. Maintain. You've *got* to reunite Nelia with Andy's kid – that is the mission."

"Did *you* get us out?"

"Andy went to bat for you. Other friends I didn't even know you had went to bat for you. I've tried to calm everyone down, not overplay this hand. Everyone's combined efforts *could* have turned you into a gilt-edged hostage. What do you need now? You got cash?"

"What I need, Collie, I think, are my immigration volumes. Can you call my legal assistant Ruth Ann and have her send the entire set DHL to this hotel?"

"Done. Anything else?"

"Tell the Goldens we love them."

"Well they love you, Shane. Andy thinks you're a stud. Let's keep him thinking this way."

The next call was from Coy 'Cadillac' Coffin.

"Holy Shit. Holy Shit. Little Rumplestiltskin wasn't up to the task." He wanted to put distance between him and the adoption certificate. "There's is a Gulfstream jet waiting at the international airport to bring you back safely. Get in a cab and *go now.* This damn thing is costing me about five grand an hour."

"Can't do it, my brother – can't leave the client here. She doesn't have a visa."

"FUCK that woman, Shane (well, you DID!) You must

be out of your mind. I could give a flying SHIT where this woman goes. From what I understand, that lady is NEVER getting back into the States, not with the way this thing has been fucked up – my Dad called Senator Percy and told him to spring your ass, Percy reported back that it would be tough – you had been charged with murder – some lady companion has been charged with murder – but somehow, YOU ARE OUT AND FREE. But they could grab your sorry ass again ANY MINUTE. You could be in a stinking Mexican jail FOR LIFE! According to Percy, this isn't over by any means. Not by any means."

"Can't do it. Sorry, send the jet back. Can't thank you enough for your efforts. Don't know how long it's going to take for me to get her some kind of visa. She still doesn't even have a passport."

"So – there you are. You are going to hang with some illegal alien and get yourself fucked. OK. Look – I'm your only real brother even though you don't HAVE natural ones. And it's been a full time job – not to mention expensive and heartrending – to BE your brother. And now, I have spent God knows how many thousands of dollars timing the arrival of this damned jet and now you won't take it. You won't take it. You are a just a suicidal shithead. You've ALWAYS been a suicidal shithead. If that's how you want to play this, I'm out. My family and I have done everything we can." In fury and frustration, he slammed down the receiver.

The final phone call came from Andrew Golden. Collie must have reported to him. He didn't ask what I intended to do, or how it would get done – he didn't establish deadlines. He never mentioned Sandy Golden. He was a *mahatma,* mining brain candy instead of salt. He simply declared that 'these things can happen' and asked me to 'protect the President' in my dealings with the United States Consulate in Mexico, whatever that meant. 'The influence ended with your release.'

I was now, again, very much on my own.

CHAPTER XXII

EN LA FONDA DEL RECUERDO

Nothing happens in Mexico City on the weekend except a sigh of relief that five more days have passed and preternatural fear that another five are about to begin. As it happened, we were released on a Friday. I had lost total track of the days.

On Saturday morning, I took Alicia to breakfast, alone. Huevos rancheros and a glass of fresh orange juice never tasted better, of that you may be sure.

I told my poor paralegal, who still had circles under her eyes darker than the La Brea Tar Pits, that I was sending her back to San Francisco. Her home was in Modesto. I told her that we were still very much under threat, and I owed it to her to get her back to her family, safely.

I told her she must also meet with my wife, now no doubt tearing her hair from its roots like a Witch of Karres, and calm her down. Nelia and I agreed to continue concealing the provenance of Esmé. Even if I were not in the best of shape, I told her, I would continue to fight the good fight. She balked at this. She wanted to see the thing through. Somehow, the poor thing thought it was all her fault.

"I can be helpful," she argued, "Your Spanish is not so good and you have a long way to go before we can ever get Nelia a passport."

But I would not be swayed. In those days, airline companies actually had offices where one could buy tickets. Pan Am kept one inside the Maria Isabel Sheraton. My American Express card still breathed virtual life: I used it to buy first class ticket on the Pan Am flight one way to San Francisco, that evening. I preserved the safety of one less human being in my hands, and that was all, at the moment, I wished to accomplish. We thought it best that she slip out of the hotel after dark in a crowd of other tourists scheduled to leave at the same time (and on the same flight!) and get on their tour bus. A small *mordida* to the driver of the bus could ensure this. She was so nondescript she would never come to the attention of the 'toads' (*sapos*), as Nelia insisted on calling the members of the secret police who kept hanging about, apparently hoping for a break in our security. We knew this to be true because we saw a pair of their wretched Camaros in the parking lot. Alicia finally agreed.

It slowly was becoming Saturday night, for Chrissakes. I was feeling stir crazy. The Marines could not have been nicer; of course, they watched our every move, and Alicia's departure was cleared, first with them and then with the Embassy.

I asked the hotel concierge, "What is the best restaurant with real Mexican food in this burg?"

"La Fonda del Recuerdo, señor!"

The 'modest restaurant of our memories'. What an appropriate place to take the mother of my illegitimate child, both of whom I had put at such risk.

I asked the Marine Guards if they were comfortable escorting us to dinner outside the hotel. They had to check with their superior in the Embassy, but it was arranged: we would take the hotel limousine, which could pick us up in the subterranean garage, and they would accompany us to downtown Mexico City, where this wondrous dining establishment waited.

La Fonda del Recuerdo did not disappoint; centered around a large courtyard with a fountain containing brightly colored fish. I ordered the most powerful margaritas I could conjure, insisting on my fail-safe recipe; I determined to get Nelia blasted, though when I knew her she didn't drink – except Bilisters, as I remember. She sure as hell did that evening, downing three margaritas in quick succession. We consumed two large orders of *queso fundido* while the Marines, looking on, nervously sipped at their Coca-Colas next to us. It was lucky we had them. Not two blocks from the Maria Isabel Sheraton, after we had left the confines of its basement, a pair of unmarked Chevrolet hot rods showed up, tailing the Marines. I wondered what our escorts might do: turn on them and take out their tires with AK47s? I hoped so. But they were as cool as their crew cuts. Once safely at the restaurant, they walky-talkied a report, to someone.

Nelia began to relax. She was wearing yet another Nolan Miller original gown that Missy had sent down to Chihuahua with Alicia. And heels. I wondered what she had in mind. I looked like a midget walking behind her, the Marines not much taller. We made a curious foursome.

"I liked your hair when it was longer," I told her.

"What do you think, I look like *una lesbeia*? This is the hair of a working girl, Inevitable Man. I took Sandy for swimming in the pool twice a day and it is a pain to try to dry it, because Missy expects me to look respectable in my white uniform."

"So. Was Esmé's a difficult birth?" I asked timidly.

"Is that the kind of question you ask your *wife* when you are trying to get her drunk?" she countered. "Esmé would not be around were it not for that asshole that pinched my *chi chis.*"

"Well, he got his."

"Yah, it's sure you broke that bloke's jaw."

"No. What I mean is, after they left, the day before – well, the day before we got together – they stopped for fuel and a little medical attention in Mexico City before going across the Pacific to Molokai."

"And then?"

"And then, there was a thunderstorm and severe wind shear on approach to the airport in Kalaupapa, Molokai, and the damn pilots put the Gulfstream into a mountain, killing all of them."

"And, if it hadn't been for trying to rescue me, you would have been with them?"

"Something like that. What goes down comes around."

"Dios mío," she exclaimed, "you live a charmed life."

"When I found you in the black cat of a *bodega*, I counted the one on the door going in to make sure he did not represent the last of my nine lives. I thought, for a moment in that jail cell, that I must have counted wrong."

She belted down another margarita as though there would be no tomorrow. "Don't form anything in your imagination, Mr. Inevitable; you are not going to do to me tonight what you did eight years ago."

For once, my imagination was innocent.

I ordered the thickest, rarest beefsteaks on offer at *La Fonda* with green-sauced cheese enchiladas on the side. We devoured them. The Marines ate hamburgers.

"So what is your plan, Mr. Inevitable? I suppose you have to get back to your family. I am happy enough if you put me on a bus to San Ignacio, as long as those *sapos* don't follow and try to cause more trouble for Esmé and me."

"I am not leaving you here, Nelia. The plan still is to get you a passport, a legal visa back into the United States, and then get you on that damned train with the Goldens and Sandy. Sandy."

"That will be when, as they say in one of your pop culture *basura* films, '*monos*' will fly out of my butt."

"A *mono* is what?"

"A monkey," and she laughed behind her hand, a reassurance she would not get on a bus and disappear.

It was daylight savings time, or some version of it in Mexico City. One of the conditions of this little outing was that we would be home by dark. A Marine respectfully pointed to his watch, and the door.

Early next morning before dawn, Alicia left the hotel on a bus full of tourists and was soon on the wings of the wind, to safety.

CHAPTER XXIII

IN THE EMBASSY OF THE UNITED STATES, MEXICO CITY

Nelia was as good as her word; wouldn't let me touch her; I didn't really try – there is a rule that lawyers are prohibited sexual commerce with their clients – I believed there must be some NAFTA provision exempting me, since I had once fathered a child with this one, but why stir the cauldron of ethical violations already brewing? At least she didn't bolt.

So I had time on my hands and spent Sunday researching my immigration books, which arrived DHL that morning, for some loophole that would allow a stateless person, or at least a person *sans* passport, to obtain *some* kind of United States visa. There is, of course a provision in the immigration law for political asylum – but Nelia was not a political person and there was neither a pogrom nor revolution going on in Belize – there was nothing to fight over.

I found a few cases allowing for special visas for purely humanitarian needs – and then it came to me – the threat against Esmé Fitzgerald nee Squalor, made to Nelia in the jail, presented plausible grounds for humanitarian intervention – and it *just might* result in reunification of mother and child in the United States.

'Collie' Green had given me the number of the consul who discovered us in the jail – Buck Gogarty – and I called him as soon as the consulate opened on Monday morning. He actually answered the phone.

After a few pleasantries and my expression of thanks to

him, he said, "Mr. Fitzgerald, my colleagues and I are dying to know – who the *hell* are you, anyway? And what do you think you are doing in Mexico? You have an interesting set of friends."

"Luck of the Irish, consul – we can discuss that later. But for the moment, I need your help. My client, 'Ms. Doe', who as you know was arrested with me, needs a visa in order to get out of here."

"Unfortunately, we now know all about 'Ms. Doe.' The United States attorney in Los Angeles is weighing his options: off the record, what could you have been *thinking* using an actress as a stand in for the marriage nullification hearing? There is no hope in hell of her getting her a visa. And, in any event, she doesn't have a passport – she would need a passport before we could even *consider* granting her a visa. And she won't be able to get one."

"But assuming she had a passport, you would consider her application. Right?"

"We are required to consider *any* application for visa which comes through the door, but as I hope I've made clear, she is not eligible for a visa. We know she was working illegally for Mr. and Mrs. Golden. We assume that if she is admitted to the United States she will violate the terms of her tourist visa and continue to work, and it would take months to process an application for labor certification. Such a certification would probably not be granted because there are thousands of women already in the country legally who would jump at the chance to work for the Goldens."

"You have to admit the marriage nullification procedure was a pretty trick."

"I don't know, what is your law license worth? We have already been contacted by the State Bar of California asking for any information we have concerning this entire fiasco."

"And?"

"We told them nothing. You are still the guests of the United States Embassy in Mexico and we protect confidences. But you, my friend, need to get *out* of here. The Mexican government, depending on how the cookie crumbles, could still send an arrest warrant to the Consulate. None has yet been received, but if it is solely directed to the fraudulent adoption certificate, we would have to honor it. The ambit of our protection has limits, Shane. And frankly, I am getting tired of calls, on the hour, from your college roommate. He is insisting you leave, and has your best interests at heart. So," and he reached into his drawer, "here's a ticket on Pan Am's flight to Los Angeles, departing this evening. I strongly suggest you be on it."

"And what am I supposed to do with Nelia?"

"Let her take a bus back to Belize, where she came from."

"No sale, Consul Gogarty. You have your mission, I have mine."

And I left the consulate disappointed and empty handed.

CHAPTER XXIV

IN THE EMBASSY OF
HER MAJESTY, THE QUEEN,
MEXICO CITY

That evening Nelia and I dined in the hotel, and she told me the story of her life: the sense of pride in her Pancho Villa heritage, the history of the tiny country of Belize, and its overthrow of the British yoke of colonialism, facts I never knew before, of course. I told her it was a pity she had never visited London. "Why the hell should I want to visit London," she said, "these guys only tried to keep us in slavery." She was a rebel.

Earlier that day, we sent money orders to San Ignacio for the support and care of Esmé. We discussed the likelihood of the *sapos* taking reprisals against the child. Naturally, Nelia wanted to return at once, to protect her. 'You sent *Alicia* home', she reasoned. But the guys in the Camaros seemed to have lost interest in us; they were no longer parked in the vicinity of the hotel. I persuaded her to give me a few more days.

Then, after dinner, sleepless, tossing and turning, tangled in my empty shroud of magic tricks, it came to me: if Belize was once a British colony, Nelia's forebears were once British nationals. It gained its independence, what, a decade ago? *Nelia was born a British national!* If I shared this weird story with the folks at the British Embassy, would someone be merciful enough to give this poor woman a passport? British like kinky.

The next morning, when the British Embassy opened, I presented myself at its door. I was interviewed by a pretty consular officer; not surprisingly, she knew everything about the Manuel Buendía murder and the fact that three innocent Americans had been charged with it.

"I am sure," she said, "that the Ambassador will want to meet with you."

I returned to the hotel to wait for her call.

The phone in my room, littered with legal memoranda, notes, and open textbooks, rang at 2:00 p.m.

"The Ambassador would like to invite you for cocktails at the embassy at 6:00 p.m. Can you manage to wear coat and tie?"

I did better than that. I bought a pin striped black suit off the rack, a white shirt, and a Countess Mara tie. It fit beautifully. I was so goddamned thin. Nelia picked out the cravat, which was dark blue with little escutcheons on it. I would charm this 'old school' ambassador.

This guy was already three sheets to the wind when his butler guided me into his study, which was a large room with a wooden ceiling of interlocked Moorish squares.

"These fucking baboons," he said by way of Etonian greeting. "Neville Henderson," and shook my hand heartily.

He powered down another gin and tonic as his valet brought me a *Cuba Libre. Muy fuerte.* Had the bartender been instructed to use half rum, half coke?

"You must be knackered after four days, wasn't it four days? . . . In one of their little *posadas.* Did they knock you about, interfere with the two women?"

The Ambassador dressed in an old-fashioned dinner jacket, one of those quilted things with black satin lapels. Right out of Hitchcock. There are pictures of Churchill in precisely such a costume. Ambassador Henderson wore patent leather slippers and a bow tie. His hair was slicked back like Noel Coward's and he peered at me over a set of half-readers. A rather substantial looking dossier on a credenza looked like it might have something to do with me. He sported the proper Oxonian accent, and I learned, in researching him later, that his father was Lord-so-and-so, their lineage traced back to Cromwell. It was like being interviewed by Hugh Hefner, but without the buxom blonds. The valet who brought my rum and coke was a churchmouse-sized Filipino.

"I'm fine, sir," I said.

"I knocked back three GT's just reading about you. These miserable cads. You know, the Mexican hierarchy is as rotten as Stilton gone bad. And it's bad to begin with. Hate the stuff. They are capable of anything. Did they hit up the Goldens for a large *mordida*? If not, you were all lucky. Perhaps not, because your Gipper got directly involved. Told old Gavin to give 'em the what for. Delicious. I would *love* it if Maggie gave me the clearance to take on some of these bastards. I *hate* this assignment. I *hate* the fucking Mexicans. I *hate* fucking Mexico City. I *hate* their Mexican food, which is nothing but silage handed down from the Aztecs. You probably feel the same. Are you actually a *friend* of Ronald Reagan?"

"No, sir, I've not met the President – but I share your views about the Mexican booreaucraps. I would like to blow that jail and everything in it to kingdom come."

"Ah, well done, young man – they didn't break your spirit. Well done. Now I *think* I know why you're here, but tell me in your own words. And leave nothing out. I love a good story; don't get one often. Your attorney-client confidences be damned – it's probably all in the file there, in any event. Pretend you are B. Traven."

"Ah, a man of letters."

For all his *bonhomie*, this guy was sharper than a serpent's tooth. I had the distinct impression if I falsified even the slightest aspect of the story, or omitted anything he might deem material, I was cooked.

So I gave him the unvarnished truth and didn't spare myself the lash. He took no notes, just listened, slack jawed, and didn't interrupt. I even told him about Esmé.

"The life of a savant is full of epiphanies, isn't it so? Churchill believed in black swans. So the kid they threatened is *yours*. How do you feel about that?"

"You don't want to know."

"I probably fathered a few bastards knocking about Africa in my early days in the Foreign Service. A black woman will never call you on the kid, considers it just wear and tear on their personal equipment. Africa's all right, because you get what you see. Here, everything is shiny varnish, pure crap beneath. Pure crap!" he emphasized. "So that's it. You have told me everything. Are you scared?"

"Frightened to death. Frightened for the client, frightened for Esmé, frightened for my marriage, frightened for my law license. More frightened about what U.S. authorities may now do, as opposed to the Mexicans."

"Bollix. Your wife is an American? Even she can't be that pedestrian. The Mexicans will drop you like gangrene once they've got what they want. I would suspect no one in the United States bureaucracy is about to take on a fellow who only acted in the best interests, in the final analysis, of a child, a man who *appears* to be a close friend of the President. Even though he may not know you from a lump of coal, he clearly had a strong interest in seeing you released without harm. That is sure to carry weight with anyone who wants to give you your comeuppance for . . . what did you call it? – Reckless lawyering. Now the Bar in California is a different matter. Now *there's* a police state!"

"I feel badly that I could have brought this to a very bad

end."

"But you didn't. You still are on the wicket. Your decision to confront the *bandidos* in the hotel room was stellar. Had you not done that, you would not have shown them *duende* and would have all been beaten to death. While they were trying to escape, you understand. Dead culprits for Buendía's assassination are more valuable than live. So. What can we do for you? The least I can do for you is grant your client a passport. I will direct the Consular Office to do that tomorrow if you will simply fill out this form." He took several preprinted sheets from the dossier. "Return with two passport photos. Don't make her look too glamorous this time." And he smiled.

"You're kidding, sir."

"No. young man. It is my pleasure to become a chapter in this unfolding saga. My only condition is that you will say something nice to Maggie about me, copying it to Reagan (for my file); in the hopes they might pull me from this sewer. The Embassy in Austria would be nice; then, at least, on the weekends, I could ski Gstaad."

CHAPTER XXV

IN THE EMBASSY OF THE UNITED STATES, MEXICO CITY II

Now, I was really on a roll. That, of course, as we have learned, is when one becomes most vulnerable – when hubris, no longer just prowling, no longer riding sidesaddle, gallops full tilt toward the goal, when its hoof is most likely to encounter a gopher hole and catapult the rider to earth. But sometimes, rarely . . . right after one has escaped death . . . hubris will carry the day.

I filled out an application for American tourist visa for Nelia – it needed exhibits, because it called for, among other things, sexual history, crimes, political allegiances. Even in the 80s it was the policy of the INS to exclude homosexuals; thus, my famous case of The Reluctant Lesbian, reported on elsewhere.

Nelia's application required recitation of her previous indictment, even though the case had been dismissed. It asked for 'contacts' sufficient to guarantee the applicant's return to her native country. Esmé was such a contact. But it also made clear that if a visa were granted, it would carry no work permit. I made no bones about the fact that Nelia needed to rejoin her charge Sandy and that she would receive compensation for so doing. This *beso de muerto* of legitimate visa applications is so profoundly silly, since we suck in illegal aliens like sand crabs at high economic tides, and cruelly expel them during economic lows – the laws of man be honored and those of God be damned – the Romans played the same game and their captive minions joined the Huns in retribution.

Somewhat hungover from my séance with Ambassador Henderson, I presented the application and the British passport to Consul Gogarty next morning.

"How did you pull *that* off, Mr. Fitzgerald? Don't tell me. I don't want to know. You are lucky that Ambassador Henderson recognizes a fellow madman when he sees one."

"Why don't you adjudicate the visa application as if it were filed in 1973, when Belize achieved its independence? There was greater freedom of movement across borders in those sunny years. Less political correctness – Oldsmobiles even came with chromium tits."

"You know I am going to have to deny this visa. You and I both know she will work for the Goldens, receive compensation. I just can't do it under the present laws, and the present laws govern this application."

"OK. I anticipated this. Buck, I can't leave here without her. So. I researched my immigration books, and found a case that says she can be given a sort of political asylum. Buck, they threatened to kidnap her kid unless she would sign some trumped-up confession. She and her kid are, even according to you, still under threat from these guys. So can't you give her some kind of visa based on humanitarian necessity?"

He considered this. I handed him a three-page affidavit setting forth the nature of the threat and the photo of Esmé as Exhibit A.

"This is not a bona-fide political asylum case. I can't do it."

"And I refuse to leave this god-awful place without her."

"You are serious?"

"Serious as a heart attack, in fact, and I hate to threaten someone who helped save my ass from those thugs, but if you don't issue my client some kind of visa by tomorrow morning, we will both take the bus to San Ysidro and I will carry her on my back across the checkpoint. If the INS grabs her, seeks to exclude her, fails to admit her, whatever, I will file for political asylum/humanitarian consideration right there on the spot. We will not slink in the shadows like the usual wetbacks. Golden's public relations firm will have Los Angeles Times reporters and photographers on hand to capture the action. If I'm going to lose my state bar card, then I'll go out in style, protecting my client to the last."

"You wouldn't do that," he sighed. "Yes, you would. You would. You are clearly that crazy. All right. I am required to report this threat to Ambassador Gavin and my counterpart at State in Washington. And, as they say, I will get back to you. So good day, Mr. Fitzgerald."

He rose from behind his gunmetal grey government desk, dismissed me by mopping his brow with one hand, and gave me a somewhat helpless but clearly respectful wave goodbye with the other.

.

CHAPTER XXVI

ON BOARD
The Fantasy Island Express

I didn't get a chance to look at Nelia's passport again until the Pan Am 727 had lifted off the tarmac of Mexico City's international airport. Gogarty and his staff granted not one, but two "C" visas; I had not even known such animals existed, but they were so-called 'Transit' visas, which treat the holder as if he/she is not really in the United States. It is intended for travelers who are stranded in the United States during a transnational stopover and need to spend a night in a hotel outside the airport. So the first "C" visa would admit her when we landed in Los Angeles, and the second "C" visa re-admit her after the trip to London and Paris. They were carefully circumscribed; the first "C" visa was good only until June 19th, the day the QEII embarked New York for Southampton; the second "C" visa was good for one week after the Goldens returned. What would happen then was anyone's guess.

What I would do with this poor creature at that time was as yet unknown, but she was good for the next sixty days, the length of the combined train-and-ocean-liner odyssey, plus a week.

I hadn't a clue how legally to keep her here. Divorce my wife and marry her? It sure as hell wouldn't be fraudulent. We had a kid. Divorce might be inevitable, in any event. But perhaps, I should just turn in my law license like an unsuccessful detective turns over his badge and gun in the movies, and refer her to other counsel.

No matter what, I believed I would have to obtain independent representation to attempt to keep her here and get a working visa. I was no specialist in those, and had run out of tricks.

But to flesh out the story: as soon as I returned to the hotel from the Embassy, we were informed by the Marine Guards to pack our things; we would be leaving late that afternoon. We were otherwise confined to quarters until they came for us. We departed the Maria Isabel Sheraton in a black embassy car followed by the jeep. No one told us our destination, but Gogarty and one of his colleagues met us at the airport when we arrived and, without inspection or exit stamps, we were bundled onto a Pan Am 727 aircraft waiting on the tarmac. Gogarty walked into the first class cabin with us; he would take no chance that I might change my mind. He only handed me the passports after all the other passengers were on board and it was time to close its hatch. "The happiest day of my life, thus far, is putting you on this airplane, Fitzgerald."

We drank a lot of champagne on the flight, celebrating our good fortune in leaving the tainted soil of Mexico, and when the plane landed at LAX I wanted to kiss the black asphalt.

We were told by the stewardess not to disembark with everyone else; I assumed I would be taken into custody by either the State of California or Federal officials for my sundry crimes, and looked for a string of police cars. Instead, unbelievably, the usual trio of white limousines appeared on the tarmac. Andy Golden stepped from the first car and greeted me with a bear hug as I stepped from the plane and Sandy, who had been informed he would be seeing his Nanny again, was bundled into Nelia's arms.

We were examined neither by Customs nor by the INS; such was the power of someone who controlled seven hours of prime time and offered his beach-house to the President.

The first limo peeled away with Andrew Golden, Nelia,

and myself on board. I gave Nelia's passport to the driver of the third limousine, who was going to pick up a visa waiting at the French consulate in downtown Los Angeles. I noticed that we didn't catch the San Diego Freeway North but kept going east on Century until we reached the Harbor Freeway, then north to downtown.

"You are in for a bit of a surprise," Andrew Golden chuckled.

The *Fantasy Island Express* rested on its own track at Union Station in downtown Los Angeles. It was composed of eleven cars inclusive of two engines: a sleeping car for staff, a sleeping car for the children and their attendants, a sleeping car for Mr. and Mrs. Golden, a dining car, a kitchen car, an antique Pullman coach owned by Lucius Beebe, a baggage car, a car containing a working office for Andrew Golden with a satellite disc on top, and a caboose.

"We are taking no chance that anyone might change their mind about you and Nelia," said Golden, puffing away on his pipe, "so we are leaving early. Our first stop will be Emeryville, California, where we will leave you off to rejoin your family. Don't worry, you won't have to be part of this circus after that. Once we drop you off, we will go through Reno, Nevada, Provo, Utah, and Glenwood Springs, Colorado, until we reach Chicago. Then we will have to change engines to a different railroad that will bring us to Washington D.C."

"Unbelievable," I said.

"And . . . Mandy has arranged a celebratory luncheon on board and you will be asked to say a few words. You are quite a hero to the Golden family, my boy, so prepare yourself." And to himself he muttered, "Jesus, this operation has become expensive."

After we boarded and the train departed the station, I was left to myself in the Lucius Beebe Pullman where a white coated butler uncorked a bottle of Tignanello, and handed me a glass and a legal pad. Golden went to his office to work and the rest of the family reunited, I presumed, in one of the sleeping cars.

So I wrote them a little poem to commemorate our adventures South-of-the-Border, which I shall share with you now:

The Saga of Nelia Doe

CANTO I

Let us go then, you and I,
to a land where smog obscures the sky,
not from cars or limousines
but from the hookah pipes of agents
wrapped in greedy opiate dreams

Let us go through certain security patrolled streets
to the glittering retreats
of producers, movie stars, and your sundry plastic surgeon
(with prices exceeding the roe cost of Russian sturgeon)
to the dwelling of a family plus unique,
and their upscale life tres chic.

For it is here the tale of Nelia Doe begins
not on some fantastic island, dynastic mansion
or floating bordello
(What is the name of that producer fellow?)
Or does it really?

For Nelia hails from a fly speck called Belize
noted for its vacant deserts and aggressive fleas
(the deserts and fleas represent poetic fabrication
solely intended for the reader's delectation.)

Actually, the place is rather pretty
in a jungly sort of way;
there are tropical rain forests,
an occasional pristine cay,
but its physical beauty masks an economic blight
and therefore, for its natives,
not a single U.S. visa is in sight.

For a Democracy based on Equality
the reasoning is funny:
Uncle Sam extends no welcomes
to equals without money.

Nelia hailed from the rural state of Cayo,
her wits her only wealth,
save some mangoes growing in the Bayou.
(Note how the poet "cayo" and "bayou" subtly blends
perverting horticultural laws to meet his ends.)

Nelia Doe wished to improve her economic lot,
and without giving the U.S. consulate a second thought
forded, a la bracero, the Belizean border
leaving behind a little child
with a muscular disorder.

Greyhound carried a tearful Nelia
through the jungles of the Yucatan
and then, North to Mexico
where she barely had a moment to hatch her D-Day plan
by which she meant to penetrate the U.S. border
and avoid the forces of so-called "law and order."

Ah, Tijuana!
Its very name rings
of garbage heaps, clapped out Señoritas
and burros doing evil things.

Nelia was stashed in a squalid motel
while coyotes sniffed out la frontera
to see if all was well.
Ten days dragged by,
of brackish water
and less than haute cuisine
causing bouts of flu and gastroenteritis
almost buying her a visa for the celestial scene.

At last Nelia began to cross El Grand Desierto
with a murderous coyote.
She had to blow away her coyote
beneath a Joshua tree
to save her compadres
and set them free.

CANTO II

But Nelia didn't drown in the L.A. basin,
– our heroine ain't no fool –
(we should strike that word from our poetic grammar
even looking like a pusher can land one in the slammer)
she was discovered, not at Schwab's or Ma Maison
but while cleaning out the Goldens' pool.

A rare talent with children was soon revealed
and Missy demanded live-in care;
Nelia's fate as a nanny was quickly sealed
and soon she became a family member extraordinaire.

For two full years thus she toiled,
changing diapers, enforcing naps;
her charge was always loved but seldom spoiled
except by a doting Daddy (perhaps).

For Andrew is a man who stays close to earth,
his flights of fancy launched by telephone,
while Missy longs to sail the ocean in a Cunard berth
navigate the Thames, stroll the Bois de Boulogne.
The problem was: how to get Andrew to New York?
Enter the ombudsman who looks like a stork.

He and his accomplices hatched a plan:
a sumptuous railway car, no less,
to make Lucius Beebe look like an also ran;
at one end a caboose, at the other two locomotives;
and to whet Andrew's media appetite
a mobile phone, fired by laser satellite.

But a dragon reared its head to spoil this pleasant scene,
and dealt a scaly blow to set the trip awry.
Nelia was, as they say, 'an undocumented alien'
and could neither sail, nor rail, nor fly.
A shyster lawyer induced her threatened deportation
to God-knows-where –
certainly, some third world nation.

To a cad named Scales she secretly wed
in pursuit of the carte vert,
a drunken stooge from the neck up dead.
His absence at an I.N.S. appointment caused a red alert.
Nelia became wanted by the I.N.S. computer,
and as soon as she could be caught,
from the country they would boot her.

CANTO III

But Missy was determined to keep the group intact
for the ocean voyage so long planned.
For the Goldens to achieve the impossible is a routine act,
so she imported the mouthpiece
of the hopeless and the damned
to rectify poor Nelia's plight.
They would not crumble to the Feds without a fight.

This mouthpiece had resolved a hopeless case or two
before,
of the tycoon who fled the I.R.S. for Zurich
to escape a tax of ten million or more;
till an aneurysm made him passing sick.
The lawyer had to spirit him to and fro DeBakey
without the I.R.S. or I.N.S. suspecting something flakey.

Then there was the case of the girl of Sapphic persuasion,
a gentle Swiss Miss from Lausanne.
She slipped into Manhattan for an innocent liaison,
but the love letters in her purse condemned her to the can.
The lawyer prevented her pending deportation
and she yet thrives in San Francisco
with the Pepsi generation.

But there never was a case, you know
so fraught with challenge and unanticipated risk,
as the insoluble problem of Nelia Doe.
The secret to success was as delicate
as a recipe for Lobster Bisque.
But the client was so lovable and fun
counsel would move heaven and earth to get it done.

Seven separate steps had to fall in perfect place.
One false move would land Nelia in the drink.
First: a computer hard drive to erase.
(not so easy as one might think)
The second: a marriage to undo
as if it never happened,
and vanish the certificate, too!

The next four moves were done at record speed,
things went deceptively smooth, as miracles go,
Nelia's berth on the QEII seemed guaranteed –
until the trio left for Mexico.
You see, to get IN this country you first have to go OUT –
one of the many ridiculous things the law's about.

CANTO IV

After Nelia's narrow escape from Mexico
it is surprising she went back at all.
But clients foolishly do what lawyers say
and Nelia bravely scaled again the wall.
(It really was a bridge between Juarez and El Paso,
Nelia hidden in a cab to escape the Federal lasso.)

In Mexico City D.F., just inches from their goal,
the three amigos were set upon by thugs
who styled themselves as Interpol
seeking out furriners as scapegoat murderers
and purveyors of deadly drugs.
For the latter crime the trio was clearly liable,
having on their person a controlled substance, the Bible.

Nelia and Alicia were taken to their room,
searched, abused, and terrorized.
The lawyer, facing jail and certain doom.
leapt within to keep the pair from being brutalized.
Their captors slapped a gun upside his head
and said, in Spanish,
"One more move, and you'll be dead."

These sapos slit the bed and disemboweled the lamps,
threw open suitcases and bags,
condemned Nelia as a transvestite vamp,
dubbed the mouthpiece and Alicia her fags.
After stealing money from the mouthpiece
and recording a false tally,
they confiscated his Sheriff's badge, snarling,
"Uno falso federale!"

The trio was cast into the cold and stony
in wretched isolation, quite alone,
their documents branded as phony.
Their captors bragged: "for murdering a journalist
You will atone."
When Andrew was alerted he ladled on the juice,
and in a few hours, his people were cut loose.

Several well-meaning folks bade the lawyer flee,
"To hell with the girl," was their unofficial plea;
but no way would the lawyer exit Mexico
unless Nelia, too, were allowed to go.
A British passport was cleverly arranged,
and the lawyer's promise to leave
for a visa was exchanged.

So the lawyer and his clients
turned tragedy to triumph
in a clever way.
Some Irish luck, and legal acumen
assured Nelia a permanent stay.
So as the group is now ensconced about this train
they depart with all the love and good wishes
of the lawyer, who will remain.

CHAPTER XXVII

FINALLY,
THE NARRATOR IS ROLLED

"Painting is poetry and is always written in verse with plastic rhymes, never in prose.
Plastic rhymes are forms that rhyme with one another or supply assonances either with other forms or with the space that surrounds them;
Sometimes, through their symbolism, but their symbolism mustn't be too apparent."

~ Attritbuted to Pablo Picasso, Life with Picasso, Françoise Gilot

I became full tired of writing this sometime this afternoon, in Todos Santos, Baja del Sur, where I escaped after I paid for the cleanup in Mexico City. You can imagine what that must have been like. Do you know me well enough now to understand that the torture trinket of a prison and the monsters who ran it had to go? Do you imagine I did not discover who the *real* killers of Manuel Buendía were, and that, like little Crusader Rabbit, I clawed and fought to bring them to justice?

Who would ever think to search for me in a country in which I had been indicted for murder? Clever, no?

One becomes a survivor after divorce, disbarment, financial ruin, prostate cancer, and immersion in a technoculture, which knows no mercy. Alcohol is a good solvent.

Too many tide pool creatures have ripped away serial pieces of me and there is little left. I had some help narrating this story; before I let Nelia escape to the mango plantation purchased for her by the Goldens as a going away present after eighteen years of service, I had her record parts of *her* story in a pearl recorder. That is a little device which had magnetic tape in it. They are now antiques. Every leaf on every tree now can have a chip that does the same thing. Your own iPhone can record you and you'll never know it!

And I do miss Nelia. I know *you* must miss her more.

But 'no *cwyning*!' as one of my little girls once said. I am now a classic co-dependent, dangling upside down above the gates of hell, suspended like a bat, or Iberian ham (you select the image) from the seat belt of a 1994 GMC suburban. I just bet it will be my last car. You can tell how many years have elapsed after our little adventure South-of-the-Border by my crass allusions to technology. Some of you techno-geeks who have never been accused of murder must be happy that I will soon be removed from the chess-board.

There are a million souls dancing on the coals of my dying subconscious: Nelia, our child, Esmé, who is now in the high corn, her husband, whose life I like to think I saved, four wives, as many children, the clients, the judges, the jurors, some automobiles (they have souls, too) – if you at any time imagined my character as unbelievable, well, listen up, you are about to be given a cook's tour of the cracks and crazes of my enamel.

You see, when you become a participant in your own case rather than a simple conduit, or umbilical, or mouthpiece, or whatever, you begin to lose, in this order, your independent judgment, your integrity, any trust you may have gained, and, finally your identity. In due course, your soul becomes the ultimate victim of such hubris.

There is a fine line between *compassion* for a client – which is a necessary ingredient of client trust – and a fiery descent into the *passions* of their case. There is a mirror in the soul, which reflects the suffering of others, a mirror, which is only accessed by empathy.

But one can easily drown in the mirror, as did Narcissus in his pool. Nelia says something about this on one of her tapes.

It was a bad idea going on that bonefishing trip with those boneheads – it was sure to end in disaster, and it did. It did. It was a bad idea entering Mexico to rescue Nelia – it was sure to end in disaster, but the tragedy turned into many triumphs. But not for me. For now, I am swinging upside down. In a car. If a suburban is a car. Well, it has South Dakota license plates that say '*Cuidado*'. That should tell you everything you need to know.

Cars are sweet coffins in which to live or die. Coy taught us that, early on. In the old days, their dashboards were like altars from the old Latin mass, hinting at intricate secrets. When you entrain the masses with architecture, organ music, vestments and words, you own them, and like sheep, they can only bleat nyyyyyyyyyah, nyyyyyyyyyah, nyyyyyyyyyyyah. Cars became tabernacles. I wonder at what speed Coy set the cruise control of his celestial starship?

The elegantly simple instrument panel of old cars did not betray their mysteries with bleats, beeps, or bells. Getting one to start was epiphany enough. One had to *guess* at a car's ailments. The cocoon of privacy they afford accounts in part for their singular popularity. Their illusion of motion, of autonomy. Apart from hallucinogens, they are the ultimate escape mechanism. Probably chrome and candy apple red coffins could have been obviated had 50s cars been equipped for the afterlife. I rather like deaf mute cars, with mohair seat covers, that can silently cruise the Wee Villa Market, the Poppy and Piute preserves, the few little towns that continue to have a core.

I can barely mumble, which must be a good thing. It brings me comfort from the pain. I may be losing my long and short-term memories. Speechlessness would conjure Chaplin, who always conjures Picasso. Does a stutterer stutter in his mind? Picasso said of the 'little clown' that when Chaplin grew older, less athletic, grey, he lost the magic of his mime, a loss coincident with the arrival of the talkies. I reflect on the fact both these narcissists used women as canvases, or, perhaps, as filters or storyboards for their art. Their artistic friction left successive conquests pregnant. I suppose my life pattern was no different. I am glad Esmé was spared – who knew me least of my various little girls. I attended all of their graduations though, even hers – from, of all places, Harvard Law School. Anonymously. I hadn't the courage to confront her.

And of course, you want to know about her beautiful mother, one of the only instances where a lawyer represented a client against his own malpractice insurance. So, the claim was: this daft lawyer designs such brilliant strategical vectors that his client ends up being charged with murder by the *federales*. Way to go, counselor.

If insurance adjusters, rather than paramecia, had populated primordial seas there would be no human or other distinctive race: like carp in the warm waters of Lake Powell, they are not only easily deceived, but absolutely clueless when skewered by arrows from compound bows. So the insurance adjuster to which my claim on behalf of Nelia was assigned, simply cut a check. A large check, which was used to set up a trust for Esmé's support and care.

What happened after Nelia stepped off the QEII when the circus animals returned from their vaunted voyage? Nothing, at first. I of course had by then hired John Lennon's lawyer, the great Professor Leon Wildes, to 'normalize' Nelia Doe. She was of course picked up by the INS eight days after returning to Los Angeles with the Goldens. Missy went ballistic. Wildes busted Nelia out.

As an inducement for her to stay in the United States, Andrew Golden arranged for Esmé's legal immigration; set up a second fund to educate her through graduate school.

That led to interesting consequences. So my little girl was well fixed.

When Nelia was picked up, I received a waspish, threatening call from 'the Fixer'. What did anyone expect – that after all that, the United States wasn't going to take action against her? But he got his in the end. Money took care of everything. Paper bags of money began circulating through California soon after we were released from prison in Mexico; some of them went as far as San Francisco.

A dollop of it paid for a law license burning party before the State Bar boys could get anywhere near me.

Some grace notes on the minor characters who populate this work: 'Collie' retired and became a columnist before he could be indicted. 'The Fixer' wasn't so lucky: he was swatted from his perch on the California Coastal commission after he accepted a bribe to vote for some desecration of the Coast (by a Malibuan!) and spent hard time in Folsom.

They say if you remember the 60s, you weren't there. Coy 'Cadillac' Coffin fit that paradigm. He became, of course, a seller of Chinese herbal medicine, in one of those pyramid schemes invented to prey upon the fears of those who believe everything they eat, breathe, and drink is poisoned. As if he needed the bread. He eventually became one of Romney's largest contributors. As in, Romney *fils*. And as for *La Habanera*, God only knows what happens to women like that – they become old toothless hags in shawls hanging around outside pueblos banging little clay cups on the sidewalk, I guess.

Brandy Golden became a truly awful actress except for her appearance in one movie starring the incandescent and onomatopoeically named Parker Posey, wherein she more or less plays her dumb Jewish blond self, and brings it off rather well. She is now some kind of innkeeper, and has very little to do with her ridiculously successful brother, and of course, nothing at all to do with her Mother.

Andrew Golden eventually went to his reward toasted with accolades from those whose careers he made.

Oh, oh!

I can hear the surf detonate on the hollow aquifer beneath the beach at La Cachora like mortar rounds over Bagdad. The sub must have rolled over and over until it wallows in sand. A record earthquake in Atami may mean something to the future of nuclear power, and the bombing in Libya guarantees $5.00 a gallon gasoline, but neither means squat, a tinker's damn, half a farthing, in Todos Santos, other than a tide which seems to be rising, at the moment, higher than usual.

This rollover is preposterous. I need only walk half a block to some organic vegetable stand, which is all the truck I can eat now. Well, that is not the complete story – I remember now. That far away tsunami made a few dents in the strand at Los Perditos Beach, and I picked up some corbina. Intended to eat them but went for the Herradura instead. And that led to my mounting, as it were, '*Cuidado*', in search of cougars. They populate the little casitas above Todos Santos.

Before I check out, you will want to know if my vengeance matches my stupidity. It goes way beyond. I used some of the massive fee (my last) from the Goldens to hire a team to blow the detention facility, in which we had been detained, to kingdom come.

Zorrilla, the chief of the Mexican police who offed Manuel Buendía, was convicted and sent to a Mexican federal penitentiary where he was stabbed thirty times within forty-eight hours of his arrival. I harbor no guilt for these hits.

But back to now. I must have rolled this suburban just after two quarts of *anejo* brought the pretty-faced cougar, who had been stalking me at what they jokingly refer to as 'social events' here, to her knees, up in Las Tunas. She nodded off before her fangs could penetrate my flaccid *pendejo*. Short and long-term memories burned out like one of those vacuum tubes in radios from FDR's December 7th Pearl Harbor address. Is the cougar a brief memory or just a fantasy?

I wonder if this latest rollover is a *mescalito* moment, or the result of a pothole encountered during flight from the cougar. It must be admitted the cougar has sculptured jowls, illuminated by Book of Kells vellum skin. Were you to prick her, she might bleed like the canvas of Dorian Gray. I think I remember her lids growing heavier. I recall golden light, perhaps from the sunset piercing the belly of a Damiana bottle; it must have been drained by sunset, projecting crystal ball shadows on the orange wall of the cougar's *logia*. The cougar believes such reflections foretell the passions of the coming velvet night, as the morning's rumpled satin sheets might reflect the woof and warp of the moon's last gasping ecstasies. I remember the slow roll of the Suburban, flexing like a sowbug and its dying gasp. And now, as I may have noted several times I am hung from the seatbelt like one of those Barcelona hams. I am a ham. Did I read her my poetry last evening? I cannot remember even that. Cannot recall one of my poems, which once drove my will to live. They held great promise, or, more likely, harbored hidden viruses falsely guaranteeing freedom, a duality, which all poetry artfully conceals.

My iPhone is no longer monochromatic; wears a nice frosting of gore around its Cyclops eye. I must have cut the web between thumb and forefinger during the rollover, gripping it like one of the Titanic's life preserver. It is a goddamned magic carpet, no? It provides the only illumination in the passenger cabin of the Suburban. I can barely see the tongue of sand creep forward through its shattered front window each time a wave detonates. I don't have a lot of time – I suppose I could use this thing to call

'Triple A' (not the alcoholic cult) in Mexicali, 1600 kilometers away, but that ain't gonna do a lick of good on La Catchora Beach. But this pint sized Polyphemus has utilities, and one of them allows for voice recording. And it is on! There is a little seismometer, or blood pressure gauge, or whatever, with a needle that is bouncing around. So, if someone has the brains to charge the thing after I kick, or if I can send a text message to someone announcing that the last bit of this novel, which has become naught but a Mobius band anyway, is *recorded*, we might have ignition.

Alrighty, then, I know how to keep awake, how to piece this together. I *do* remember each of my cars, in succession, and the women and circumstances that accompanied them! *They* are the milestones on the Roman Road of Life! But we bore you with all of them.

My 1958 Morris Minor, turquoise blue with grey interior, all ninety horsepower of it, with seats which did not fold back. Had they done so, my life would have been much different. I probably would have become a suburban workadaddy. In fact, since it *looked* like a baby buggy it was perhaps too anthropomorphic, certainly lacked the muscle tone, to score with babes. I do remember chauffeuring this clapped out Franciscan, allegedly the world's expert on Junipero Serra long before it was discovered he beat the shit out of the Indians and may have butt fucked some *niños*, to LAX. He had just delivered a speech to the student body to inspire some of us to become new missionaries to the pagan babies, perhaps in Malawi, and for our reward (undisclosed), we could have used stepladders to pleasure Masai women and quaffed blood mai tais. Over the clattering, self-destructive 4 cylinders of the Minor's engine, we heard the news of John Kennedy's death, and Walter Cronkite's choked voice on the radio, and the death of our dreams.

But an editor would say: what does this segue about your claptrap have to do with the story-line? And he (or she) is right. But I am dying, for Chrissakes, and when you are dying, this is the type of shit which passes before your eyes.

So get used to it.

There is no visibility now from the shattered windshield of the suburban, and small waves of sand seem to be groping their way further into the passenger cabin. They must be pushed by the damned rising tide from the typhoon.

Oh. The sand appears to get the better of me. It has now risen to my lower lip, and my head compresses the headliner of the roof. I can smell the acrid aroma of dying sand crabs, or something. This silica will soon French kiss my tongue and compress my lips I hope it doesn't crush the iPhone.

In any event, I have uttered much more than I should have ever wanted to say.

CHAPTER XXVIII

AT THE 100TH ACADEMY AWARDS

"What have we here?" shouted Jeeves Regal into the microphone, "Mr. and Mrs. Sandy Golden have arrived in a vintage Morris Minor 1000 Woody Station Wagon. Driven by a gaucho complete with sombrero and Emiliano Zapata moustache. Only the Goldens, who live on the remote Hawaiian Island of Ni'ihau, would dare emerge from such a contraption. The crowd roars in delight as they step onto the red carpet. Sanford Golden is the only son of the legendary producer Andrew Golden. As you may know, the notoriously private Goldens do not grant interviews, but this year Golden Productions is up a for an academy award for best film for *The Saga of Nelia Doe*. In fact, the movie has received an unprecedented eleven nominations, not only for best film, but for best leading actor and actress in a feature role, best sound, best art direction, best score, best film editing – and it has already swept the Golden Globes. Mr. and Mrs. Golden, a word please."

The sun poured down on the couple, he in a conventional Brioni tuxedo, she in a simple white Navajo shift with embroidered bodice. Sandy Golden slowly shook his finger at the interviewer, smiling: "As my late father might have said, let's not jinx this thing by brushing the dust from the butterfly's wings."

"Any comment from you, Mrs. Golden? You co-produced this film with your husband."

But Sandy held Esmé Golden in the sweep of his left arm far from the microphone, and by the time he made his comment, the couple had moved forward beyond its range.

"Mrs. Sandy Golden is one of the more interesting women in Hollywood. Still on crutches from a childhood illness, they say she has mesmerizing eyes. Those are her eyes you see in the Esteé Lauder ads. All of the royalties from the use of her image, worldwide, are given to charitable causes. The couple certainly doesn't need the money. He is now the largest shareholder of ABC, with a net worth of over 25 billion dollars. But they are indeed the subject of great mystery; no one has ever been able to trace the ancestry of Esmé Golden; her records at Wellesley College, where she was Valedictorian, and at Harvard Law School, where she was Editor of the Law Review, are not made available to the public. She and President Barack Obama share birth certificate secrets. Some people say she grew up in the ultra secretive household of the late Andrew Golden; others say that she comes from a banana republic in Latin America, and was brought illegally into this country by her mother, who worked as a maid. There are multiple rumors as to who her father might be, and Mrs. Golden does not say. The couple met at Harvard Law School, where she became the first woman editor of the law review and the only person of color, since the President, to hold the title. But this movie is said to give answers to some of these mysteries. We shall see! This is Jeeves Regal, on the red carpet, signing out. Back to you, Louella!"

The Goldens were shown to their seats in the center of the tenth row. Esmé would much prefer watching the sunset from their secluded home on Ni'ihau. There, the only glitter floats off the waves of the Eastern Pacific, reflected by the wings of Sandy's collection of live butterflies, the largest in the world, or from shimmering hummingbirds feeding on fuchsias in her atrium of orchids. A childless couple, the flowers, hummingbirds, and butterflies would be their legacy to the world. But they had decided to do this film together, as a tribute to her parentage, so often pilloried in the press and gossip columns.

"Were Nelia alive, do you suppose she would be proud of me for doing this?" whispered Esmé to her husband.

"It's hard to say. She was proud, I think, of anything you accomplished. But she was at heart a simple woman and hated working in California. I remember when I was little, she made wooden toys for me: just a top, a kind of carved wooden spoon for sand at the beach, and a carved crab with claws that actually moved. I loved them so much, more than all the garbage from the box stores."

"And what of my Dad? What do you think he would have thought about the film?"

"Do you mean, do you think the film is true to his book? He would have to tell you that, I think. Again, hard to say. I have mixed feelings about him. He took tremendous risks in his life, but relied on others to pull him out of trouble. Though he risked everything to pull me out of trouble, I guess. I remember Mother, when she was alive, complaining that she had to bring a shopping bag containing $100,000.00 in hundred dollar bills to some thug in South Los Angeles in order to rescue your Mom and Dad from that Mexican jail. But Mother complained any time she had to spend money which was not purely voluntary; we didn't put that part in the movie. Your Dad would probably admire you forsaking law for film-making – anything to get you out of lawyering for a living! From the book, I take it he considered such a fate more deadly than suffocating in quicksand."

"I wonder if the scene where my Grandpa blows those Mexican secret police to kingdom come is a little too bloody. A little too Quentin Tarantinoish. I remember it as if I were there now, my simple, humble, quiet Grandfather. I never even knew he kept a shotgun in the *palapa* – pulled it from behind the rafters hidden by thatched palms. He fell to the floor as quickly as a cat, then two rapid explosions, each blowing *chayote* sized holes in the chests of those cowardly men. I can still smell the gunpowder, see the men collapse in the darkest part of our hut. It took several *abuelas* days to remove their gore from the bamboo walls; another used seven pails of water and a bar of soap to wash the bone fragments and blood from my hair; my Grandfather either fed the rest of them to the catfish in the Macal or buried them so deeply in the *huerta* they would never be found. "

"What was the working title you gave that scene? *Wholly Communion?* That may offend the Catholics. Of course, all the members of the Mexican secret police were raised Catholics. But they deserve our depiction of them."

"So, overall, what do you think – what do you really think Sandy? – did we do a good job? Are we going to bring home the roses this evening?"

"Ah, my dear, the only roses bloom on your cheeks," said Sandy, giving Esmé a kiss.

"They are just little gold men, Esmé, little gold men. From the box office results, I would say that we did a *very* good job, indeed. Every Hispanic person, in fact, every person of color in this country who is illegal, has been deported, or suffered at the hands of the Immigration Service will want to see this film. Because, in the end, it is a film about hope. It is not just, as my Dad might have said, eye candy – it has substance."

"Do you suppose they ever got together again after he left her on that train that took you to Washington, and then, Europe?"

"You always ask this question. You are such an incurable romantic, like your old man. You know, my Dad bought her that mango orchard in Belize. The one she left to you. I haven't a clue what happened after that. I don't know if he ever visited her there. I know that Nelia never spoke about him to me, not once. I remember meeting him again, though, and you remember that from our graduation from Harvard. He left right after you went to the podium. And he said the most interesting thing – which I have never told you, because at that time you were in your 'I am woman hear me roar' phase – and you were resisting marriage – he said that we were the result of an 'epiphanic inevitability.' I am still not sure what he meant."

"He *was* a romantic," sighed Esmé, "certainly a great but unrecognized poet. Nelia saved his poem from the train; that is why I added it to the script, even though poems aren't read in movies any more. I often dream of them as lovers – my Mother used to tell me stories about Pancho Villa's steed, *Siete Leguas* – and Pancho riding with La Avitia in the sagebrush outside Chihuahua. My Mom went to Chihuahua to chase down the ghosts of her Villa ancestors, and then my Dad went to chase down my Mom, not even knowing who or what he would find. He didn't know they had made me. I see my parents sipping strange drinks in that weird bar, *El Gato Negro,* in Chihuahua, rediscovering each other beneath a portrait of La Avitia. In many ways, they were romantic revolutionaries like Pancho and Avitia."

"I hate to remind you that in the book there were only beers served in that old bar. Are we going to allow the movie to be streamed on Netflix and all that?"

"We are not even going to let them *digitize* it, Sandy! It belongs on celluloid, like an old romance – like Steve Spielberg says – now watch the screen!"

Suddenly, the chatter in the theatre ceased. Sandy Golden put his fingers to Esmé's lips. She kissed the buds of his fingers. The golden hologram of Oscar faded from the stage. The curtain rose. Fabricated of silk damask, it drew aside and upwards in baroque folds. One could almost feel the vibration of the antique Wurlitzer.

The title of the first nominee for best picture, *The Saga of Nelia Doe,* was projected on an antique screen, beneath the logo of Golden Productions: an exploding, reverse spiral supernova with stardust filaments sifting down through an ebony sky, signifying a river of passion and pain, turning into snowflakes at nightfall, drifting toward a tiled, dark-raftered, ruined adobe.

This tableau had been abstracted from a painting by Jules Tavernier, an artistic member of the Bohemian Club of San Francisco. Tavernier kept the painting hidden during his lifetime. After his death from alcohol poisoning in Honolulu, it was found unframed in his personal effects, and purchased anonymously from his estate by Sandy and Esmé. It belongs to that rare genre of oil paintings known as 'nocturnes'. The original was donated and returned to the Bohemian Club, in exchange for an exclusive license, in perpetuity, for use in Golden Production Company's logo. Because, as it was later claimed, all tableaus created by Bohemians, for use in club shows, are ultimately the property of the club.

It now hangs on a southern facing wall in a foyer outside the club's main loggia. The adobe's asymmetrical windows, like the eyes of Plato's apocryphal soul, are dimly lit by mesquite fires within. If one stares at them long enough from a distance of about three feet away, one may experience a green flash of the type sometimes accompanying a Pacific sunset.

Esmé sees in the ancient structure's windows the green eyes of her ancestor, La Avitia. She likes to believe that, though the original structure of Tavernier's inspiration has probably crumbled into dust, it might, on some special starry night, be re-discovered, glowing, somewhere in the desert of northern Mexico, perhaps not far from Chihuahua, Chihuahua.

FINIS